Love Not Required

Ginny Vermillion

Copyright © 2013 Ginny Vermillion
All rights reserved.

ISBN: 1484003993
ISBN 13: 9781484003992

IN MEMORY OF THE CHILDREN
OF MY HEART
BETH ANN HAYDEN
AND
DOUGLAS Q. VERMILLION JR.

Chapter One

Going crazy. Going bankrupt. Going home.

Not as she would have liked. There was no pleasure in humiliation no matter what Charles had said. "You can't take this personally, Josie," he had told her. Easy for him to say. "The climate isn't the same now. Jobs are at a premium. You'll get a topnotch recommendation, I assure you. Under no circumstances are you to think this had anything to do with what Jason did. You aren't going to cry, are you?"

She had wanted to. Her tears were used up. Jason's fault or not, he was dead and she was saddled with his disgrace. To say nothing of the mess he had left behind.

"You don't need to feel responsible," Charles had said, clearly expecting she would.

"If it takes the rest of my life," she had insisted, "I'll pay back every penny he stole."

Charles gave her a first class ticket, a firm handshake, and a repayment schedule the size of the national debt. A list of possible job assignments once she was back in the states had already been prepared for her. From the looks of the waiting area, the flight was full. The seats around her were no longer empty as they had been when she arrived. Being early was habit. Besides, she had no place else to go. To pass the time, people watching was her only amusement. The collection of passengers appeared to be the usual assortment of business and pleasure travelers, talking or reading before boarding. Only one other person seemed to be doing exactly what she was doing. Their eyes met briefly. She looked away.

Strange. Even with a quick glance, she could usually recall at least one feature of someone she had seen. Oddly enough, the man she had just looked at had left no impression on her at all. Nothing.

Glancing up at the clock on the opposite wall from where she was sitting, she looked at him again. He was leaning against a pillar. The stance was casual, but she got the distinct feeling he was far from relaxed. Maybe she had spent too long sizing up immigration requests. Her job had required sharp instincts. Outward appearance aside, the object of her curiosity was definitely on the alert. She wondered what for.

With a well trained eye, she studied him. Tall, probably six foot plus. Sandy blond hair, conservative cut. Smooth shaven, no visible scars on his face. The set of his jaw spoke to her of a man in command of himself. He had a neat, proportional build somewhere between wiry and angular. Nothing about his clothes conveyed more than the fact he wore them well. The brown slacks had a crisp crease and the tan jacket, tweed she thought, fit well over his broad shoulders. The results of her appraisal were inconclusive except for one thing. The guy was sexy. Definitely sexy. Not wanting to be caught in the act of giving him the once over, she looked back at the clock. Early boarding should begin within minutes.

She would wait for the last call. She always did. When the final announcement was made, she finally started for the Jetway.

The yawning entrance to the plane was a familiar reminder that flying was not among her favorite pastimes. Safety aspects aside, aeronautical details had never quite explained to her satisfactorily what kept that huge machine from falling out of the sky. To top it off, the seats were uncomfortable, she rarely had any interest in the movie being shown, and inevitably whoever sat next to her provided about as much entertainment as a pelvic exam.

They either said nothing or too much. Maybe this time would be different. With that thought in mind, she reached the door to the plane.

One look into the first class cabin told her lively repartee was probably not going to come with the ride. The one feature of her sexy stranger she had not been able to see from a distance registered instantly the minute she slid into the seat next to him. Perhaps piercing was an overstatement. Penetrating definitely applied. The umber color was dark, almost to the edge of blackness. This time his eyes held hers and she did not look away. There was something about his look that came close to being seductive. Either she had been deprived for too long or he had a flair for turning grown women into mush.

"May I take your coat, Mrs. Giltner?"

The voice of the flight attendant reminded Josie that first class travel came with a personal touch. It also gave her an excuse to look away from her unsettling seatmate.

"Thank you," she replied, looking up at the woman with hanger in hand.

"May I bring you anything before our departure? No? Mr. Angelus, how about you?"

"Nothing," he answered, in a short clipped tone that bordered on rudeness.

"I'll check later," the woman assured them both before going off to deftly deposit Josie's coat in what looked to be an already full hanging locker.

He had a slight accent. Not foreign. Definitely American. One word was insufficient to place it, but she had unmistakably heard the cadence. Whether or not the sharp edge to his voice was usual she had no way of knowing. In spite of those fantastic eyes, maybe he was a grump.

Just what she needed. A man with an attitude to add an extra touch of irony to a trip that didn't have much to recommend it in the first place. Maybe he would fall asleep and not wake up until they reached New York. All she asked was that he stay off her case. If he had some problem with that, he had better keep it to himself.

※ ※ ※

Had she been sent to keep tabs on him or was his imagination in high gear? How clever to assign a woman. He knew most of the men. She wasn't what he would have expected. While looks could be deceiving, her slight frame did not suggest the stamina of being able to survive the obstacle course, much less the rigors of yearly endurance tests. Hell, he'd almost blown that himself less than six months ago.

Examining possibilities, word had it there was a new program that was less strenuous in an effort to increase the female work force. Didn't she know better than to request a seat next to her subject? Had the training program sunk so low? Her appraisal of him had certainly been sloppy. Long before she checked him out, he had already sized her up along with a good number of other passengers as well.

She stood out because she didn't fit neatly into a category. A tourist? He didn't think so. While it wasn't unheard of, few women vacationed alone. There was no evidence of business trappings. Her small bag was inadequate to hold a laptop and there was no overstuffed briefcase or additional luggage. As a rule, business people tended to push the limits of carry-on restrictions far beyond acceptable levels so they wouldn't lose time retrieving luggage at the end of their trip. What immediately came to mind when he first saw her was a stereotypical trophy wife.

Nothing about her was out of place from the top of her well-coifed head to the tips of her manicured nails peeking out of the open toes of her shoes. Her pale, translucent skin contrasted sharply with the blue-black hair. Finely sculpted facial features had the look of being crafted by a master plastic surgeon. Dressed in a navy blue suit with a white tailored blouse visible between the lapels of the jacket, her jewelry was all understated and obviously of the best quality. As an extra touch, they had even thought to have her be married.

In fairness, he should be flattered. Such a lovely choice to soothe his way back into an environment he was more than willing to concede had become quite alien to him.

"We're in a new age now, Stephen."

He could hear Thaddeus speaking as clearly as if he and not she was sitting beside him. Yes, times had changed. Drastically. What rankled him was the presumption he, of all people, needed assistance. And by a woman no less.

As far as he was concerned, he had only one choice. Calling her bluff might not be the mark of a gentleman, but she must have been told he was a son of a bitch.

"Why were you checking me out?"

Up close, her face was even more startling. To his surprise, she looked embarrassed rather than defensive as he had expected.

"I didn't mean to be so obvious." Score points for good acting. She appeared to be genuine. "It's a nasty practice I picked up in my job."

"How did I measure up?"

"To be honest, from a distance, there isn't much to distinguish you from any number of men fitting your general description."

He didn't bother saying he hadn't earned his reputation by drawing attention to himself. The fact she was studying his face more closely than she should now was a gaffe he would report once he was rid of her. Anyone with such singular violet blue eyes was headed for extinction in their line of work anyway. To amuse himself, he would see how well she had memorized whatever cover she had been given.

"What kind of job do you have?" he asked.

"At the moment, I'm unemployed. I used to screen applicants wanting to immigrate to the states. They were an interesting bunch."

"I'll bet.

"Some were positively ingenious. Since I'm not doing that anymore, I suppose there's no harm in saying the dishonest ones were actually the best part of the job."

"Did you quit?"

"I'd like to say yes, but the truth is I became expendable. At least I wasn't the only one. Some people lost career positions. My reason for being there was far less noble. The lure of European living had me under its spell."

"Didn't they offer you something else?"

"There's nothing available and spell or no spell, I'm a realist." God, he couldn't deny she was convincing. "My time there was more like a gift than anything. The man who got me the job no longer has any influence and the climate is so different now. My dreams of living out my days in a quaint villa on the Mediterranean have suffered a setback, but that may be just as well."

She sounded sincere without looking for sympathy.

Although his circumstances were not as drastic as she pretended hers were, he saw no reason to hide his bitterness when given the opportunity to vent it. Neither would she if her situation was real. Where, he wondered, was a husband supposed to fit into all of this?

"These days two incomes are almost a necessity," he ventured, opening up the subject if she wanted to tumble for it.

"Especially if you like to eat," she replied.

Her face told him he had struck a chord. Exactly what that meant, he didn't know.

"Have you decided what you'll do next?" he inquired. She must not have her facts on the husband thoroughly mastered.

"I haven't a clue. I think my chances are best at home."

"So you're leaving Europe behind?"

"For now. How about you? Does your business often take you abroad?"

She had a look of innocence unlike any he had seen other than on the face of a child. How much had they told her about him? Didn't she know any better than to try and put him on the spot?

"I was on a sabbatical." The comeback was automatic. If she had any sense, she'd leave the matter alone.

"Oh, I see. Lucky you."

Lucky was about the last word that came to his mind. Displaced or rescinded were close, but obsolete was more accurate.

Peering out of the window, he took in his last view of the land where a once brilliant vocation had now come to an ignoble end. Pulling the blind down eliminated tarmac activity from his sight. Then, he remembered to put the blind back up for take-off. His appointed tagalong was nervous, assuming the rigid pose of a white-knuckle flyer. Someone whose characteristics were so transparent did not fit in their profession. She belonged in a much more refined atmosphere far away from the harsh realities he wore like a second skin. As hardened as he was, he had to admit she had a certain appeal to him. Probably because she reminded him of all the things he had convinced himself were out of his reach.

She was one classy looking broad all right. Not his type, of course. Try as he might, he couldn't think back far enough to the days when he had considered a woman good for anything other than sex. Quite possibly, he never had. Women got in the way. They wheedled and connived more than not. No one had done a better job of insulating himself than he.

Still, as he looked at the woman beside him, he wondered. With her eyes tightly shut as they gained altitude, she didn't seem to care if anyone knew she was uncomfortable. He had controlled outward expression for so long, he found her openness somehow refreshing. Maybe he was overreacting. Maybe she really was simply a woman who had lost her job and was going home just like he was.

She opened her eyes and caught him in the act of watching her.

"Now who's doing the looking?" she asked

"I am," he answered. "You don't like to fly, do you?"

"Not particularly. You don't like being asked questions, do you?"

Shy she wasn't. That intrigued him.

"Is that a crime?"

"Not as far as I know. I could be wrong, but I got the impression I upset you."

Was she that inept or had he misread her? It was in his best interest not to take unnecessary chances. If she was going to be reporting his words to the powers that be, the correct approach was to keep playing the game.

"I'm not sure how I should take that," he said.

"You may take it anyway you like." He had to give her credit for not backing down. "Have I upset you?"

"No. Not at all. I'm not a very gregarious person."

"I see." Her eyes met his without flinching.

He had underestimated her. She was as capable as he at putting cards on the table. Most people found him intimidating. From the looks of her, she did not. Instead of belaboring the point, she smiled. He found the gesture more than a little disarming.

"If I had to take a guess, I'd say you really don't see at all, but you'll accept my word for it," he said, returning her smile. Damn. One more minute and he'd be flirting with her.

"You could say that, or," he could swear her smile was real, "you could say it's a long flight and it makes sense to have things as pleasant as possible."

Diplomacy became her. The job she claimed she had lost would have required the practice. What her feelings really were didn't matter. How people felt about him wasn't important, especially women. Because he believed she would be informing on him, he would behave accordingly.

"You're right," he said, hoping he sounded sincere. "I don't know about you, but I'm going to have a drink."

"I think I'll pass for now," she told him, unbuttoning her suit jacket and starting to take it off.

"Here," he said, reaching around her, "let me help you."

His hand brushed across the softness of her hair as she turned her back to him, twisting in the confined space to free her arms. He was close enough to smell the scent she wore and to admire the delicate line of her neck. In a moment of complete insanity, he imagined running his fingers along the finely textured skin to see what her reaction would be. Whoa, boy, he told himself. You may need a woman, but she's not the one.

"Thanks," she said as she took the jacket from him. "What would you suggest for a safe, neutral topic we can easily kick around without stepping on each other's toes? Or would you rather sip your drink in peace and quiet?"

The shoulder padding in her jacket had hidden how slender she was. She came close to being painfully thin. Her tactful approach got him off the hook if he wanted. On the other hand, he could try his luck at making a good impression for her to report to Thaddeus. That would fix the old coot's wagon. Serve him right for sending such an amateur to evaluate a pro.

"How about favorite cities in Europe?" he asked. "Do you have one?"

She didn't answer immediately. She thought for a minute instead.

"I have several favorites for different reasons. How about you?"

"I suppose I do too, but if I had to narrow it down to one, I'd say Rome offers almost everything."

"Over Florence or Venice?"

And so it went while he pigged out on a leg of lamb with all the trimmings and she picked at a salad. He stoutly defended Rome while she championed Florence. Switching gears, she went to bat for London against his preference for Dublin. In the process, he discovered she shared his love of history although he did not admit to his feelings for the subject. He liked the way she wrinkled her nose when she laughed and was surprised at himself because he was comfortable with her. Toward the end of the meal, she started to yawn.

"I've bored you," he said.

She shook her head. "That's not it. I didn't sleep very well last night. Having a second glass of wine probably didn't help any either."

"You sure can't say you ate too much."

Her shrug served as an answer. An educated guess said she had recently lost a lot of weight. The wide wedding ring she wore was too big as was her watch band. Putting her head back against the seat, she looked over at him.

"Sometimes when I'm lucky, I can sleep on a plane. In case this is one of those times, do you promise to give me a poke if I start to snore? I've been told I can be quite annoying."

"Leave it to me," he answered as her eyes closed. Motioning for the flight attendant to bring a blanket, together they covered the already sleeping form beside him. As he leaned over her, the closeness allowed him to see the trace of make-up carefully applied to hide the deep shadows under her eyes. Last night wasn't the only night she hadn't slept well. What had Thaddeus been thinking to hire someone with such obvious signs of strain? Unless, if he put the frustration of his current situation aside, she was exactly who she said she was.

If he took a minute to look at how paranoid he was getting, he'd realize he was hardly a candidate for observation. That process was for those suspected of burnout or case mismanagement. No matter how pissed he was by the shift in his profession, he wasn't doing anything more than changing assignments. Thaddeus wouldn't waste manpower to escort someone like him home.

Nerves. That was all it was. Facing an uncertain future could do that. Instead of preparing himself to adjust accordingly, he was looking for enemies where none existed. Like the sleeping woman beside him.

So frail. So vulnerable. So beautiful.

What was wrong with him? Was he going soft? Of course not. As soon as he got into the groove with the new scheme of things, nothing would faze him. Especially not some dewy-eyed beauty whose lips, slightly parted in sleep, conjured up visions of pleasure far beyond any he had ever known. When the plane landed, she and her dimpled smile would be gone. To meet her husband or start a new job or whatever she was going to do. She was not his problem. Getting accustomed to a drastic change would be enough to keep him occupied. He had no time for women. Distractions were not allowed. She was an interlude. Nothing more. He would forget her.

※ ※ ※

"Ladies and gentlemen, the captain has turned on the fasten seat belt sign in preparation for our landing. Please return to your seats and...."

The usual litany broke into Josie's tormented dream, pulling her back to reality. Sleep, when it came, was never restful anymore. Would it ever be again? Would she ever be the same again?

At least she had proved to herself she could carry on a natural conversation with a man. Well, all right. Maybe the present circumstance was pushing it. Mr. Angelus hadn't chosen to be with her. In the beginning, he had seemed to find her downright annoying. Then, for some reason, he had changed his mind. While not exactly a charmer, he had a definite flair for what she called Southern manners.

That was it. That was the accent. She had a knack for picking them out. Not the deep South. Closer to the Mason-Dixon line, she guessed. Maybe Virginia. Something in the way he handled himself spoke to her of good breeding and ingrained behavior she associated with many Southerners.

Not that he *looked* the part. Quite frankly, he reminded her more of the hard, bitter types at work who came to trip up the suspected criminal sorts trying to slip through the cracks. Like the men who questioned her after Jason killed himself. Men who flat out told her she was lying. Most of whom to this day probably didn't believe her. The comparison was unfair. She opened her eyes to escape the sting of memory.

"Another minute and I thought I might have to poke you after all."

His voice wasn't the least bit unkind. How unfair to lump him with those morbid souls whose ancestors probably instigated the Spanish Inquisition.

"Was I snoring?"

His smile was restrained, but the real McCoy. Another mark of Southern gentility, especially among the more aristocratic set.

"If you had been any quieter, I would have suspected you weren't breathing."

"Did you nap yourself?"

"No. I never do. I'm one of those people who needs to be stretched out flat to sleep. As comfortable as first class seats are, they just don't do the trick for me." He sat forward to look out of the window. "We're almost there," he said.

She leaned over to have a look herself. All she could see was water. Obviously unaware of her closeness, the man pulled back, nearly bumping into her. A normal reaction would have been for her to move as quickly as possible. Instead, she felt inexplicably drawn to him. His eyes held hers with an intensity of an unspoken demand not to look away. It was as if he wanted to memorize her face. The effect on her was both intimidating and exhilarating. His lips hovered over hers with mere inches separating them. Had he bent to kiss her, she could not have refused him.

As slowly as possible, she began to relax back into her seat. "Will you be staying in New York?" she asked, her voice sounding far away to her.

"No," he answered. "You?"

"I'm afraid not."

"Will your husband be meeting you?"

"I'm a widow.

People generally registered some sort of reaction. Her stranger did not. He still held her gaze as a lover might. Deep within her there was a stirring she had convinced herself had died along with Jason. Thank goodness she would not have to handle those feelings along with everything else coming at her. Forcing her eyes away from his, she reached into her purse and took out her compact. The face staring back at her in the mirror was pinched and drawn. She snapped the compact cover closed. How she looked was the least of her concerns.

"It seems to be raining," he told her. To confirm his report, a soft mist covered the window.

"So it does." How appropriate. "At least it's too late for snow."

The grinding of landing gear and whine of wing flaps sounded ominous to her. She hated landings almost as much as take-offs.

"Assume the position," he said.

"Do what?"

"Clutch the seat arms and get ready to put on your brake."

"If that's supposed to be funny, I'm not amused." She felt herself flush with embarrassment, doing exactly as he had said before she could stop herself.

"There's probably at least a dozen other people on board doing exactly the same thing."

"Just for that, I hope your customs inspector makes you open every single one of your bags and messes up the contents."

"I bribe them," he said in a conspiratorial tone. "They never even give me a second look."

"A greaser of palms, are you? I knew it the minute I laid eyes on you."

"For a price, I might be convinced to steer them away from you."

With arched brows and twisted lips, he did a great imitation of a conniving swindler. "You'd probably want too much," she laughed, rapping him on the knuckles. "Besides, then I would be in your debt."

He grabbed her wrist, deftly pretending to be twisting her arm. The contact of her flesh and his sent a surge of pleasure through her.

"I do blackmail too." He laced his fingers in-between hers. "What do you say?"

"I'll take my chances and hope for a pass," she replied, all too conscious of how his touch was affecting her.

"Pity," he said, looking down at their hands. "For a moment there, I thought I might convince you." Releasing her hand, he glanced toward the window. "We're down," he said.

"Excuse me?"

"We've landed," he answered. "That's why everyone is fidgeting to get up."

"Oh."

He had distracted her on purpose. Along with the other passengers, she unbuckled her seat belt and stood up. So did he. She had misjudged his height.

He was well over six feet. There weren't many men who made her feel petite. Not as tall as she was.

"I hope everything works out for you," he said.

"Thanks. I'm sure it will."

She wasn't sure at all. As they walked up the Jetway together side by side, the fact he had made the flight tolerable did not escape her. Any illusions that what was ahead of her would go as smoothly didn't seem worth contemplating. Squaring her shoulders, she looked straight ahead. There would be no handsome strangers to fill her horizon. At the doorway, he paused.

"Rome is still better," he said, throwing his garment bag over his shoulder.

"Be glad I didn't take off on Venice. Good-bye."

He made no reply, turning instead toward the customs area. She hoped he might, but he did not look back. Soon, he was out of sight, leaving an empty feeling inside of her.

Only one thing was for certain. Rosemary would be waiting for her. And no one filled time and space the way Rosemary did.

Chapter Two

❖

"Josie, over here, darling. I'm over here."

The unmistakable pitch of Rosemary's voice reverberated off the walls of the cavernous building. An exaggerated twang, long since adopted as her own, had no resemblance to any accent known to man. To be precise, Rosemary Armature was a self-created woman who took every aspect of herself to the most extreme limit she dared.

Reacting to the summons, Josie had no trouble picking her godmother out from the rest of those waiting along the barricade between customs and the terminal. Few women would choose chartreuse and purple for any reason, much less to wear. Nothing Rosemary did came even close to being ordinary. Nothing.

"You don't have to mess with any of those formalities," Rosemary informed Josie, as well as everyone else within earshot of them. "Come on through here, love. Your bags will be brought out as soon as they are located."

Next to the flamboyantly clad woman was an official looking man she had obviously collared to do her bidding. How he felt about his assignment was plainly etched in a care worn face used to enduring the trials of a public servant. Once through the barrier, Josie was instantly enclosed in two plump arms housing enough bracelets to make up a department store display. Garish colors, over abundant perfume and all, there was more comfort in that embrace than Josie had known in a long time.

"Wendall will kill you if you thwarted the system, Rosemary," Josie said, referring to Rosemary's long suffering husband.

"I'd like to see him try. My powers of persuasion are one of my more developed traits. Let me look at you." She released Josie enough to look her up and down. "I do declare you resemble a bean pole with bumps. It will take weeks to get you filled out, child. Give me another hug. Hot damn you feel good, even if you are all bones."

"You feel pretty good yourself. Where's Wendall?"

"Off seeing to the high knuck knuck of a place too small to show on a map with tons of oil gushing all over the place. He wanted to come, of course, but you know Wendall. Now, if you had flown into DC instead of making this silly detour."

"I told you I couldn't help that, Rosemary. Charles gave me the ticket. I could hardly look a gift horse in the mouth."

"If I had my way, that spineless twerp would be strung up by that part of his anatomy he probably spends his free time playing with. If it's the last thing I do, I'll see to it he falls from grace so hard it will take him a year to remember his name."

Rosemary had ways of accomplishing things Josie didn't want to know about. "Could you at least wait until I'm gainfully employed again? He's promised me a good recommendation."

"He should be on his knees asking your forgiveness. As to your working, I won't even discuss how I feel about that."

"You already have, Rosemary."

"If you'd just let me help."

"The answer is no and always will be."

"Have it your way. I didn't think it was possible for anyone to be more stubborn than your mother was, but I've been wrong more than once. Oh, good, here are some of your bags at last."

"That isn't some of them, Rosemary. That's all of them."

"You're kidding."

"I got rid of as much as I could. I only kept what I really wanted."

"Good Lord. I couldn't get my underwear into six suitcases. Well, so be it. Now, then, what did I do with Maxwell?"

"Don't tell me you've lost him again."

"I never lose him," Rosemary insisted defensively. "I merely misplace him."

"You generally give him distinct instructions about where he should wait for you and then promptly forget what you told him."

"Those chairs over there. That's where I left him. Go find him, Josie, while I keep an eye on these pitiful treasures you've dragged back with you. If you look closely, you may possibly see a glimmer of how glad he is to see you."

Josie doubted it. During all of the years Maxwell had been employed by the Armatures, he had maintained a stoical appearance one would associate with a chauffeur. She had never seen his expression change. He always looked as if he found the world and everyone in it slightly unpleasant. His back was to her as she approached him.

"Hi, Maxwell. The dragon lady sent me to fetch you."

A giant of a man with ebony skin as dark as the night rotated around at the sound of her voice. As a little girl, she had been frightened of him. Somewhere along the line she had realized the protection he offered.

"You're home, I see."

His expression didn't change one iota. It seemed unlikely a slightly raised eyebrow counted as an indication of bubbling joy at seeing her. The word home hardly applied. Rosemary and Wendall provided a place for her to stay temporarily. She had no home.

"I'm getting there," she replied. "If you want to get the car, I can manage the luggage."

"Would you like to guess Mrs. Armature's reaction to that suggestion?"

"Mrs. Armature hasn't had a practical reaction to whatever makes sense in the last forty years or more. Unless you're concerned about the prospects for your continued employment, why don't you and I prove to ourselves we can handle a simple situation efficiently?"

"You've grown up," he said, reaching into his pocket for the car keys.

"I've done a lot of things since I saw you last, Maxwell."

"I know." His face actually softened, or at least she thought it did. "Sometimes life hands us a heap of hurdles to get over. Nobody I know gets through it without some bruised shins."

"That's the truth if I ever heard it, Maxwell. We'll meet you out in the passenger zone."

"She'll carp."

"Have you ever known her not to?"

Carp didn't really cover it. Born dirt poor, Rosemary Armature had taken on the trappings of wealth without looking back. She was not used to having someone else take charge.

"This will save a lot of time," Josie assured her. "If you like, I can scare up a porter, but a couple of luggage carts should do the trick." Rosemary looked at her blankly. "Over there," she said, pointing to the rack of carts. "Come on. I'll show you."

Leading the way, Josie got her luggage arranged on the carts, found the elevator, and saw them safely to the outside curb. Unused to physical activity of any kind, Rosemary puffed and panted her way along, making no secret of her opinion about Josie's unorthodox method.

"You shouldn't have let Maxwell browbeat you, Josie."

"Maxwell would consider that way beneath his dignity and you know it. Here we are, safe and sound. It sure beats walking all the way to the parking garage."

"I had no intention of walking anywhere. Maxwell would have handled things. He always does."

"He also has several hours of driving ahead of him, Rosemary. Give the man a break."

"Honestly, Josie, the next thing you know you'll be offering to drive for him. I do declare. Will you look at that? I swear some people have no manners."

Josie's eyes followed Rosemary's down along the curb side. The object of her godmother's attention was leaning casually against the trunk of a stretch limousine. He was definitely ogling. No question about it. As their eyes met, he gave her a small salute along with a rakish grin.

"I can't tell you about his manners, Rosemary. He sat next to me on the flight. I would say we slept together, but he said he couldn't on a plane." She returned his smile.

"Oh my, you are naughty." Rosemary's throaty laugh rumbled through her ample form. "Who is he?"

"Just a man," Josie said, forcing herself to look away. "All I can tell you about him is he's partial to Rome. Otherwise, I don't know."

Nor do I want to, she thought, unable to keep from sneaking another peek. He was still watching her in a lazy, almost insolent way. Very little imagination was required to guess what was on his mind. Josie felt her cheeks start to burn. Another part of her body started to react as well. Thanking her lucky stars she was rid of him, the welcome sight of Maxwell pulling up to the curb gave her an excuse to break the disturbing eye contact.

"Well, it's about time," Rosemary groused. "We must have walked at least twenty miles."

"Well, ain't that a shame?" Maxwell retorted. "That's the most exercise you've had since Hector was a pup. You must be plumb wore out. Where's the rest of the stuff?"

"This is it." Rosemary replied, "and if you dare cock that impertinent eyebrow of yours at me, I'll tell Maxine to put you on bread and water for the rest of the week."

"You got a need for a driver?" he asked Josie. "This woman not only has no milk of human kindness running through her, she like to break my back every time she goes away. I swear she buys extra so she can take everything she owns and then some."

"Oh pooh," Rosemary chastised him, affectionately patting him on the arm. "Josie doesn't need you. I do."

Maxwell let that go by. While he arranged Josie's bags in the trunk, he looked over at the stretch limousine ahead of them.

"Whoever that is has influence," he observed. "Anybody else would have been shooed out of here, but nobody's bothering them."

Josie allowed herself to look again. Stephen Angelus was no longer there. She doubted he would be using such fine accommodations in any event. He didn't look like the type. Maxwell opened the door for her. She got into the back seat before Rosemary lowered her bulk into position.

"We're off," she said cheerfully. "Maxwell will have us home in no time. Now don't try to fool an old pro. That cover up you're wearing is good, but I can tell you're exhausted. You need your rest, my dear. I've planned some very informal get-togethers so you won't be under any strain."

Rosemary's idea of informal and Josie's idea of informal had nothing in common. There was no use trying to back out of whatever was planned. Entertaining was as essential to Rosemary as breathing.

"I won't be staying very long," she reminded her godmother. "As soon as I get a good offer, I'll be getting a place of my own."

"You have a place of your own with us, Josie. Don't begrudge me that."

"My reluctance doesn't have anything to do with you and Wendall. You know that."

"Of course I do, but you need more than a little pampering after what you've been through."

"All things considered, Rosemary, I'm luckier than most."

The answering snort reflected Rosemary's opinion. "You've been through hell, Josie. No question about it. You said the less said about it the better and I'll respect that. The only thing I would like to know is what, if anything, you've heard from Jason's folks since the funeral."

"Not a word, Rosemary. I didn't expect anything really. What is there for them to say? I hardly knew them when Jason and I were married. He was ashamed of them, you know. Poor people. I really feel sorry for them, but the one attempt I made to stay in touch fell flat."

"They probably thought you wanted them to help pay back the money."

"That's what I was afraid of, but I certainly wasn't going to say anything." Josie rested her head on the seat and looked out at the passing scenery. "They're back in Georgia in their safe little world. It's better that way."

Without needing to be told, Rosemary honored the unspoken need Josie had to leave the subject alone. The pain was knotted inside of her so tightly she had learned to accept its almost constant presence. A few days with Rosemary and Wendall wouldn't make the hurt go away, but she could be assured there would be no idle time on her hands. Her godparents believed firmly in living life to the fullest.

Caught up in Wendall's crushing bear hug as soon as Maxwell let her out of the car, a sense of safety settled over her. A day or two to catch her breath was just what the doctor ordered. The type of luxury Jason had tried to acquire by his deceit was an Armature staple back through generations.

The expansive entryway to their house had the look of an art gallery in keeping with each carefully appointed aspect of the vast estate. As gaudy as Rosemary was with her attire, she favored Wendall's simplistic taste in her surroundings. Each understated aspect in decor and furnishings spoke quietly of the Armature wealth. Facing a future as close to abject poverty as one could get, indulging in the good life might just help ease the blow.

"Josie, sweetheart, welcome home," Wendall boomed, giving her a final bone shattering squeeze before letting her go. "Rosemary's been in her element for weeks. I can't tell you how that takes the pressure off of me. My work never goes as smoothly as it does when my wife is up to her ears in plans. She even redid the upper guest suite in your honor. I hope to God you like yellow."

"How you do run on," Rosemary said to her husband, totally refusing to admit she had made any fuss over her godchild's visit. "The suite was positively shabby after those strange people from the republic of someplace got through with it. With or without Josie, redecorating was a must."

"I think," Wendall winked at Josie, "someone wore the nap of the carpet down below Rosemary's specifications. Actually, she had been dying to redo it ever since Madge Harley found this fabulous interior designer and put the entire neighborhood to shame."

"Fiddle-faddle," Rosemary replied, full of righteous indignation. "Madge Harley didn't discover Antoine. Evelyn Brewster did. She told Madge about him in the hopes he could salvage something out of that monstrosity she calls a house."

"She has no taste," Wendall mouthed behind his wife's back.

"Not a shred of taste," Rosemary intoned as if her husband had spoken aloud. "Antoine had his work cut out for him on that one. What is that you're fidgeting with, Wendall?"

"It's an offer for Josie," he answered, grandly handing an envelope to his godchild. "Thaddeus Muldoon is interested in her."

"That sawed off runt? He hasn't been interested in anything except work for years."

"This is about work," Wendall explained patiently. "He thinks he may have a suitable position for Josie."

"What does he do?" Josie asked.

"Government contracts mostly," Wendall replied vaguely. "Thaddeus needs someone fluent in Russian."

"Well, he can go get somebody else. Josie needs a rest before she puts her talents to use."

"He doesn't want her to start today, Rosemary. All he wants to do is talk with her. I told him she wouldn't be available until next Tuesday."

"Five days? You call five days a rest?"

"It's important," Josie said. "Thanks, Wendall. What does a girl have to do to get a drink around here?"

"Heavens to Betsy," Rosemary blurted out. "What are you thinking of, Wendall? Get the child a drink and get me one while you're at it. A double anything will suffice."

Clutching the envelope from Thaddeus Muldoon as one might a life line, Josie followed the bantering couple into their version of a family room. While quite comfortable, the entire room was filled with priceless pieces handed down from Wendall's ancestors. Rosemary's philosophy was that nothing that couldn't be used was worth having. How everything managed to survive the constant wear and tear of an endless flow of guests was really no mystery. If something got broken or wore out, there were more than enough replacements in storage to fill the gap.

Alone at last in the top floor guest suite decorated precisely as if she and not Rosemary had dictated the specifications, Josie was finally able to open the envelope Wendall had given her earlier. Curt and to the point, the missive inside gave no indication as to what Thaddeus Muldoon had in mind. The heavy stationery was embossed with the name of Keener & Cooke, Inc., a company unknown to her. Other than a date and time for their appointment, the only other information was to present the summons upon her arrival. To whom would evidently be ascertained once she got there.

It was a place to start. Unless the salary was generous, she would have to look elsewhere. In order to make any sort of dent in the sum she had pledged to repay, monthly reimbursements would need to be in the thousands. She had already sold almost everything of value she owned to start the process. There would be living expenses to consider of course. Staying with Rosemary and Wendall was out of the question. Bridges should be crossed when appropriate. First things first.

Five days had never passed so quickly. Each was filled to overflowing with Rosemary's intimate brunches for fifty people and quiet nine course dinners for twenty casually served on Limoges with Waterford crystal. The kitchen help were used to the pace, making the flow appear effortless. Josie longed for meat loaf and mashed potatoes. Instead she got truffle laden sauces and pate de foie gras. Time to look for an apartment was non-existent. She was the star attraction for people she hardly knew and was unlikely to ever see again. How silly of her to suggest driving herself to meet with Thaddeus Muldoon. Maxwell would take her, wait for her, and bring her back home. Arguing was useless.

"You got your fill of all those heavy foods and snobby people yet?" he asked as he pulled out of the lengthy driveway.

"The people I can more or less ignore, but the indigestion isn't so easy. I've never seen so much food. What I really hate is how much of it gets wasted."

"Not as much as you think," he chuckled. "Those of us out back have been eatin' purdy good right along with you."

"Well, that's some consolation. If I'm not too long, do you think we might detour for a hamburger on the way back? It's been ages since I had a really decent one."

"I know just the place," Maxwell replied. "What sort of job is this you're interviewing for?"

"Beats me. Wendall set it up. I could be in for anything from translating to counting airplane nuts and bolts."

"That should be exciting," he remarked dryly, falling silent until pulling into a parking spot about fifteen minutes later. "That building two spaces up is where you're going. The one with the green canopy at the entrance. Doesn't look much like a company to me. Better check the address."

The address was right. Once inside the door, Josie was instantly struck by the silence. A lone receptionist sat behind a highly polished desk with nothing but a telephone on it. No papers, no blotter, no clutter. Nothing.

"May I help you?"

Even the woman's voice was hushed. Following suit, Josie gave her name in a similar tone, not wanting to sound out of place. The envelope she had been given changed hands and the contents were carefully scrutinized.

"Follow me."

The thickly carpeted hallway assured the muffled atmosphere was not disturbed. Josie was beginning to think her guide was lost by the time she paused in front of a closed door, identical to dozens they had already passed. Although something surely distinguished her final destination from all of the other entrances, she was at a loss to tell what. Neither a number nor a name identified who or what was behind the door. Knocking briskly, the woman waited for a low buzz that unlatched the handle.

"You may go in," she directed Josie, immediately pivoting around and going back down the long corridor.

Cautiously pushing the door open, Josie stepped over the sill into another austere room as sterile as the reception area had been. Small hairs on the back of her neck bristled with uneasiness. What had Wendall gotten her into?

"Sorry for the cloak and dagger routine, Mrs. Giltner. It helps to assure only those people we want to come in are admitted. I'm Thaddeus Muldoon. Thank you for coming."

The voice belonged to an actor or at the very least an announcer of some sort. Rich resonance rolled out with every word as she turned to meet her interviewer. She expected a tall, good looking hunk. Thaddeus was anything but. He could easily have passed for a gnome. Nature had bent his body while endowing him with the tongue of an angel. Like the rest of him, his hand was small. His grip was firm.

"Let's go where we can be more relaxed," he said, leading her to an inner door and standing back for her to enter. "I have a most unusual request to make of you."

As inviting as the rest of the place was inhibiting, the cozy room they entered was designed for comfort. Adding to the ambiance was a gas log glowing softly in the fireplace.

"Please sit down," Thaddeus suggested. "Anywhere will do."

Choosing a barrel shaped chair she quickly discovered rocked and swiveled, Josie settled in gingerly. Thaddeus took the chair across from her.

"What I'm about to suggest to you may sound absurd," he told her. "Please be assured I am quite serious and I am willing to pay you whatever you ask if you will take the job."

That part sounded good. Now, what was the job?

"What is it you have in mind, Mr. Muldoon?"

"A masquerade, if you will. Let me explain. What we do around here is a type of private investigating for the government. The appropriate departments conduct their inquiries and when they need people to play pertinent roles, they turn to us."

"I'm afraid that's an area about which I know nothing."

"Actually, in this instance, you have exactly the experience we want."

"I do?"

"Most assuredly and you also have top security clearance."

"Wendall said you needed someone who speaks Russian."

"Did he now? That may have been more for his wife's benefit than anything else, but depending on how successful you and your partner are, your knowledge in that area could come in handy."

"Partner?"

"Of course, Mrs. Giltner. We would never ask you to do what we have in mind without an experienced colleague being with you. I don't wish to alarm you, but what we do is not without an element of risk. Shall I continue?"

"You did say I can name my own salary?"

"Yes indeed."

"Then I am most interested in hearing more."

Thaddeus rubbed his hands together in a gesture of enthusiasm. His elfin face broke into a smile.

"Let me bring the man in here with whom you will be working if you decide to accept my offer. He has been thoroughly briefed and can no doubt help considerably in assisting you to reach your final decision."

She became aware someone else was in the room while Thaddeus was talking. There was no sound of a person entering, only a distinct impression of another presence.

"Hello."

The voice was unmistakable. A tightness in her throat betrayed inner feelings she kept her face from showing.

"Mr. Angelus. So we meet again."

Chapter Three

❖

She looked good. It was amazing what a few days of rest could do. Her outward cool assurance might easily be an act. Just walking into the hallowed halls of Keener & Cooke, Inc. was enough to rattle most people. As to a reaction to him being there? Hard to say. He had certainly never considered the possibility he would ever see her again.

"Small world, isn't it?" he asked.

"Getting smaller all the time it would seem," she replied.

"Has Thaddeus been spinning stories for you?"

"Not yet. We've just been talking."

"I'll bet."

Stephen pulled a chair over beside the two of them and looked from one to the other. Thaddeus was insane. There was no way she could do what he had in mind.

"At this point, Stephen," Thaddeus explained with exaggerated patience, "I thought it best the three of us should be together. Mrs. Giltner has indicated she is interested in what I have to say. For once, I would find it immensely gratifying if you did the same."

Good old Thaddeus had such a clever way of reminding his employees who was in charge. Let him ramble. Pipe dreams never amounted to much anyway.

"Picture, if you will," Thaddeus began, leaning toward Josie, "an elaborate scheme set up as a front to disguise large purchases of arms to be sold to the highest bidder. To throw everyone off, the mastermind of the plot uses a most unlikely guise to hide behind. In a twisted sense of irony, the man is head of one of the most powerful political forces on the Washington scene. The well entrenched religious right. While espousing a strict ideology of a pathway to heaven, the man is interested only in a high stakes journey to hell. Currently he's residing in Los Angeles raising funds for the cause."

When setting up background, Thaddeus was prone to flowery metaphors. Showing so much of his hand up front was a big departure from his usual approach. No one could talk around a subject better than Thaddeus.

"This is an example of what you might be called upon to do, isn't it, Mr. Muldoon? You're not relating an actual situation, are you?" Josie asked.

Women who lived in embassy cocoons abroad hadn't a clue about how dirty politics could be. Her wide-eyed innocence was as appealing as the blush in her cheeks when he had sent suggestive messages to her at the airport.

"I'm afraid this is not a premise of a possible scenario, Mrs. Giltner," Thaddeus told her. "In the interest of time, I'm putting cards on the table I wouldn't normally show. I know I don't have to impress upon you the confidentiality of my remarks."

She looked confused. With luck, she would turn Thaddeus down. There was no way a man could work with her and keep his concentration in check. She had too much to learn.

"Are you saying that Porter Holloway is not what he appears to be?" she asked.

"You know him?" Thaddeus inquired.

"Personally, no. I know of him. His brand of religion is a little too narrow for my taste."

"If you decide to accept my offer, Mrs. Giltner, you will need to pretend the beliefs he claims to hold dear mirror your own right down to the last sinful repercussion."

"I'm not a very good actress, Mr. Muldoon. As a matter of fact, I'm terrible at it."

That should make the stubborn mule realize he had picked the worse possible candidate for such a sensitive assignment. All he had to do was look at her. She wore her heart on her sleeve. The possibility of her fooling a nitwit, much less Porter Holloway, hadn't a prayer.

"If we wanted good actresses, Mrs. Giltner, we'd hire them. What we want is your sharp instincts and observational skills. Learning a part simply takes a little training. I wouldn't think of sending you into the field without it. Stephen here is overflowing with experience he can share with you."

What Stephen was overflowing with had no resemblance to what Thaddeus was talking about. How was it possible to be aroused by someone and repelled by her both at the same time? Yes, he had plenty of training experience. None of his trainees had come close to evoking a mixed reaction of lust and loathing. She'd say no. He could take that one to the bank.

"I'm sure you know much more about what it takes than I do, Mr. Muldoon. Could you tell me the type of training I would need?"

Through half-closed eyes, Stephen watched Thaddeus outline a training regimen in such idealistic terms any ninety year old could whip through it with ease. The man was hopeless. In reality, she'd last maybe a day, if that. Endurance didn't require physical strength as much as it did the ability to disregard everything but the mission. In Josie Giltner's privileged little world, what experience did she have to draw on other than what outfit was appropriate for each date on her social calendar?

Maybe that was unfair. Thaddeus was deliberately as cryptic with her background as he was with any employee. The less known about each other the better was his catch-phrase. Not a bad philosophy to be sure. In their line of work, personal attachments were not recommended. The opposition was rarely polite in their tactics to extract information. What you didn't know, you couldn't divulge.

Breezing through his highly glossed version of reality, Thaddeus had the ability to weave just enough factual essence into his explanation to put what he was saying on the fringe of plausible. Satisfied he had gotten through the minefield successfully, he stood up with a grunt.

"Now, I'm going to leave you two alone to discuss specifics you might like to have clarified, Mrs. Giltner. Stephen has the tendency to look on the dark side of things, but don't let that distract you. That aside, he's very good at his job."

In customary fashion, Thaddeus bowed out with his look of serene composure firmly in place. It was time for a cup of coffee and several cigarettes. That gave Stephen maybe twenty minutes, tops, to convince Josie Giltner hanging by her thumbs would be preferable to working for Keener & Cooke, Inc.

"Nothing's that easy," she said the minute Thaddeus was gone. "Are you going to tell me the truth?"

She was shrewder than he gave her credit for. There was no time like the present to kiss her off.

"Regardless of what Thaddeus says, you need to keep your thoughts to yourself at all times. It isn't acting, actually. It's playing a part where the stakes are much higher than a flubbed line."

"In other words, I would be a spy-type," she guessed correctly.

"That's your terminology, not mine," he replied.

"What do you call what you do?" she persisted.

"Broadly, I'm an information gatherer," he evaded.

"And narrowly?" she pushed.

Why was he evading her? Being a spy wasn't exactly a glamorous occupation. Maybe agreeing with her would be enough to convince her to look somewhere else.

"I'm a spy."

"Thank you for being straight with me. When it comes to not showing how you feel, I gather that only applies when you're on the job." She was good at cutting to the chase.

"Basically." That sounded bland.

"So it's okay for you to make no secret about your opinion of my lack of qualifications?" My, my. She was perceptive.

"What do you mean?" he hedged.

"Come on. I may not be as clever as some, but I wasn't born yesterday. You don't want to be my partner on this venture. I get the strong impression you'd have more faith in a chimpanzee."

Sitting there in her primly tailored suit with ankles demurely crossed, she could well have been attending a tea. Only a slight flush in her throat indicated she was struggling to stay calm. Her blatant honesty had blossomed without warning.

"Don't take it personally," he said, getting up to cover his confusion. "I think the whole plan stinks."

"Because you think the plan is faulty or one of the players is?"

"Listen." If he looked at her, he'd blow it. He addressed the wall. "I've been in this business for almost eighteen years. No assignment comes with a guarantee. A general rule of caution is to reduce risk to a minimum. This isn't a game we're playing. It's life or death. Do you understand that?"

He wheeled around in spite of himself. If he broke things down to the bare essentials, surely she wouldn't want anything to do with Keener & Cooke, Inc. What he read in her eyes and the tilt of her chin instantly told him otherwise. Here was a lady who dug in her heels. Obstinacy was murder to overcome. Her voice was flat when she answered.

"I came here not knowing what to expect." He was willing to swear her eyes grew in size. "It's imperative that I find work immediately and I'm in no position to be selective about what's offered to me. You don't think I'm qualified. You're probably right. I am capable of learning, however, and you've been targeted to teach me. Whether we like it or not isn't the issue. I need the job. Do you understand that?"

Scaring her off wasn't going to work. Appealing to her common sense might.

"Tell me," he baited her, "how would you rate your physical strength? Specifically, I'd be interested to know about your stamina. How are you at making it to the finish line?"

A sensible woman in her position would admit she hadn't paid any attention to body building since required phys ed in high school. Josie Giltner had the audacity to mull over her response before answering.

"Up until a year ago, I would have had to say my closest brush with exercise was taking the stairs when the elevator was on the fritz."

"What happened a year ago?"

"My husband died."

"How?"

"He blew his brains out. I found him." She spoke as if she was talking about someone other than herself. "My way of coping with the shock was to walk. I got up to as much as ten miles a day sometimes. The habit has stuck. The daily length varies. According to my last physical, my health is good. I've never lifted a weight in my life or run in a marathon and it's been ages since I climbed Everest. When it comes to dealing with adversity, I think I know how to hang in there with the best of them."

"How do you handle monotony?" He'd try another tack.

"Excuse me?"

"Tedium. Hours on end when absolutely nothing happens."

"Impatiently."

"Then you wouldn't like my line of work."

"Liking it is immaterial," she insisted, refusing to be swayed by any sensible argument he was ready to offer. "I didn't like interviewing people who had garlic for lunch either. Each job has its own brand of drawbacks."

He was losing ground and he knew it. All he had left were low blows. A man had to use whatever ammunition he had at his disposal.

"You will be a liability."

"Not if you do your job right, I won't."

She could think fast on her feet. He had to give her that.

"I don't make any special concessions for anyone I train."

"Why should you be expected to?"

"If you ask me we're both wasting our time."

"I didn't ask you."

"You'll regret it."

"That's my problem. When do we start?"

"The specifics are our illustrious leader's domain. His usual method is to pick the most inconvenient time he can. He's put together that way. I think he has a sadistic streak."

"Don't you believe a word of it," Thaddeus broke in, coming back into the room trailing the smell of tobacco along with him. "What Stephen is neglecting to mention is our work rarely adheres to a logical timetable. Everyone always wants things done yesterday. We do our best to accommodate the impossible."

"Or invent it," Stephen growled.

"Now, now. Let's not dwell on the negatives," Thaddeus warned, frowning at Stephen. "I'd say the training should start as soon as possible. I can make arrangements for plane reservations to California without much notice."

"California?" she asked, obviously unprepared for that nugget of information.

"He forget to tell you he gets a kick out of choosing unlikely training spots," Stephen told her, enjoying the reaction.

Thaddeus ignored him, speaking solely to her. She had that wonderful look of amazement on her face again.

"We can't take chances. May I call you Josie?" Without waiting for an answer, he went on. "The likelihood of anyone knowing you is remote. We want to keep it that way. We may also require a few minor modifications such as a different hairstyle just to be on the safe side."

"Contact lenses wouldn't hurt," Stephen suggested.

"She already wears those," Thaddeus informed him tartly. "What is it you're proposing?"

"Her eyes are an unusual color. It might be to her advantage to camouflage them."

"Point well taken. A tint should do the trick. As for your assumed identities, that's being worked on. All I have so far is the names you'll be using. You may want to use them during the training to help Josie become accustomed to them."

"If you tell me they're Adam and Eve, I may consider retirement."

"Your humor is unappreciated as usual, Stephen. You will be Theodore Hartmann. Your wife is Althea."

"Wife?"

Josie's voice had a hint of a squeak. That one really got her. At least they had something in common. He found the whole set-up beyond distasteful.

"Of course, my dear," Thaddeus droned. "Peter Holloway surrounds himself with supporters who are married. It fits his image, don't you see. I'm counting on you to help this hopelessly confirmed bachelor with at least the appearance of being a doting husband type. He's not taking to the idea very kindly."

How nice of Thaddeus to mention his misgivings. She looked like she had a few herself.

"I hadn't considered that aspect," she said, biting her lower lip in what he took for apprehension.

Why hadn't he thought to tell her? Was that the stumbling block she wouldn't be able to get over?

"Every conceivable effort will be made to assure your privacy when you're not on display for Porter's benefit if we get to that point," Thaddeus promised her.

"It makes all the sense in the world," she said, obviously absorbing the shock better than her intended mate had. "At least we've found something at which I have experience. I do know how to be a wife."

"You also know your way through the suitable accouterments wealth provides," Thaddeus told her. "The Hartmanns will appeal to Porter because they both come from money. He doesn't, but he's embraced the finer things with a vengeance. Fakes he can see through mainly because he was so well acquainted with them before he hit the big time."

"I've been trained by the best," she offered as an explanation, leaving Stephen in the dark about where she fit in to the social stratum. "Where are we going in California?"

Damn. She was going through with it.

"It's a lovely spot, actually," Thaddeus clarified for her, "in the Santa Cruz Mountains, not too far from a town called Boulder Creek. Are you familiar with the area?"

"Not at all," she said.

"It rains a lot." Steven held on to the slim hope she'd change her mind.

"You've been there?" she asked.

"Several times. The mornings are foggy and the sun has a devil of a time getting down through all of the trees. Sort of dreary in its own way."

"Sounds appropriate," she said with a decidedly false sweetness. "I'm ready whenever you are. What should I take and how long do you think we'll be there?"

An eternity. "You'll need serviceable clothes like jeans and sweats." Unlikely wardrobe selections for her, he imagined. "We won't be going any place fancy. As to the time, that's up to Thaddeus."

"I'll give you two weeks to begin and a month to evaluate progress. By then, you should have developed a passable imitation of a happily married couple and Josie will have been able to grasp the rudiments of the type of scrutiny we require. Once the project begins, I can't tell you how long you'll be needed. A lot of that depends on Mr. Holloway. When do you think you can be ready, my dear?"

Such a solicitous approach. Thaddeus was especially sickening when he got what he wanted.

"Tomorrow."

Surely he hadn't heard her correctly. She must be calling Muldoon's bluff.

"That's fine. Let's say the day after. An early morning flight will get you to San Francisco where you can pick up a car. Just one more thing, Josie. No one, and I mean no one, is to know where you are."

"What do I tell Rosemary?"

Who in the heck was Rosemary, he wondered.

"Tell her you're in a training session for our interpreter program that's very intense, so you will have to call her when you can. If you can't get around naming a location, tell her it's in Seattle, Washington. That way you'll have an excuse for calling at odd times. Can you manage that?"

"Yes."

"As to your salary, I've written a figure down I hope you will find satisfactory."

He passed over a square of paper for Josie to look at. She blinked rapidly and nodded her head.

"That will be fine," she told Thaddeus, handing the paper back to him.

"Good. I'll call you with the flight time as soon as I have it. Any questions you think of I'm sure Stephen can answer for you. By the way, don't take him too seriously. Nobody else does."

With that, the bureau chief proceeded to lead her to the door. As they got to it, she turned back to where Stephen was standing by his chair.

"See you day after tomorrow."

She was incredible. He'd be lucky to get through the first week without having wet dreams and less than celibate thoughts. That should improve his temper enormously.

"Off to go shopping?" he asked, not bothering to hide his sarcasm.

"No, I think I have what I'll need. My next stop is to get a hamburger."

Carrying herself like a graceful swan moving through water, she followed behind Thaddeus making him look all the more clumsy. Stephen sat down dejectedly. His career had just reached a new low.

"That went well, don't you think?" Thaddeus was back. "I'm really quite pleased, aren't you?"

"Ecstatic."

"Next time I ask you if you've ever met a woman you think you might tolerate, don't tell me yes."

"What I had in mind with her didn't have anything to do with a crash course in covert operations. I should have known you were up to something when you fed me that line about having to take the detour to New York. The first class hook should have been my clue."

"I wanted you to meet her without being prepared. You can be charming when you want to be."

"I thought she was a plant you'd sent to look after me."

"Of all your failings, not being able to look after yourself isn't among them. What I wanted was an objective opinion. You said yourself she appealed to you."

"She did and she does. You're taking a big chance putting me with her in that little mountain nest you call a cabin. I may end up chasing her around the bedroom."

"You're too much of a professional for that, Stephen." Thaddeus was so naïve at times. "What will come through, I think, is how you follow her with your eyes. A man who loves his wife would do that."

"I want to bed her, Thaddeus, not marry her."

"As it turns out you'll do neither, but you will work with her."

"What happened with her husband?"

"She told you?"

"I need to know, Thaddeus. My life may depend on her stability. I don't like surprises."

"Jason Giltner was an accomplished con man who slipped through the cracks of the background check that got him his position with the ambassador to France. By the time he killed himself, he had fleeced a goodly number of people with an ingenuous phony art scheme."

"It's odd he didn't run," Stephen said. "His kind usually do."

"Oh, I think he was planning to. His greed tripped him up. By the time he was ready to fly the coop, the exits were barred."

"Where did Josie fit into all of this?"

"You might call her his biggest mistake. He took on excess baggage he shouldn't have. By all accounts, he was crazy about her. He also thought she was wealthy."

"Isn't she?"

"Not as all."

"What about this Rosemary person?"

"Rosemary is Rosemary Armature, a doting godmother, Stephen. Her family was quite ordinary."

"Was?"

"Her parents are dead. She is an only child."

"Did she know about her husband?"

"No. She was taken in by him like everyone else. I think even more so, if that's possible. I must say she handled herself admirably. Letting her assume the entire debt seems heavy-handed to me, but she wouldn't have it any other way."

"So, you're helping her out, are you?"

"Absolutely not. The truth is the only chance we have of pulling this thing off is for you to be as convincing as she is. You're good. Very good. You've fit into your roles without apparent effort because shadowy figures aren't display items. How you interact with Josie is crucial. You know as well as I you have no experience to draw on for this one. She tapped something in you and I don't mean your voracious carnal appetite. You were comfortable with her, Stephen. We need her. Not the other way around."

Thaddeus had a way of rationalizing none of his underlings had ever found a way to dispute. Stephen knew better than to try.

"Maybe she'll choke on that damn hamburger," he said.

"If she does," Thaddeus replied, "we'll just have to find you another bride."

He was doomed.

Chapter Four

❖

"You're going so soon?" Rosemary flounced around the sitting room in Josie's temporary suite, genuinely upset at a development she had not considered. "Wait until I get my hands on Wendall. No matter what you tell me, he's at the bottom of this."

"I'm not sure what his role is, but I feel fairly certain he wasn't the instigator. You have to keep in mind, Rosemary, that training sessions are usually scheduled months in advance."

Thaddeus had said no one was to know where she was going. Other than a false destination, he hadn't provided any tried and true approaches for sounding plausible. Even if he had, Rosemary would have been just as difficult to convince.

"I don't care," Rosemary pouted, sitting down heavily in a wicker chair that groaned from the impact. "I had so many more plans I won't get to see through now."

"Of course you will," Josie told her. "No one does a party like you do."

"It won't be the same," Rosemary insisted. "The parties were for you."

Putting down the blouse she was folding, Josie went to her godmother's chair. Memories of the mother who had given birth to her were dim and faded. Her main source of comfort had always been the spoiled, indulged woman whose sense of generosity, while often misplaced, was nonetheless sincere. Admitting how scared she was couldn't be done. Kneeling down and putting her head in the familiar wide lap of solace went a long way toward making the future seem a lot less daunting.

"I have to go, Rosemary."

"No, you don't. This whole business is totally unnecessary." A pudgy hand brushed at her hair, soothing some tension away. "You need to have a life, Josie, find a husband, and settle down."

"My one stab at that didn't turn out very well, Rosemary."

"That's because you insisted on living like a gypsy, too far afield from the solid prospects you should have been considering."

"Like Martin Markley the fourth, or is it the fifth?"

At each carefully arranged affair, Rosemary had slipped in one or two eligible local specimens she considered likely contenders for Josie's interest. Most were pleasant enough, but not apt to show undue attention in an atmosphere so transparently contrived. Except Martin Markley the whatever he was. Josie put him in the certifiable jerk category.

"He's extremely good looking." An important requirement in Rosemary's opinion.

"I've known very vain women who handle their looks better than he does, Rosemary."

"He has more money than he knows what to do with." Yet another top selling point.

"So he told me. I must not have shown the proper admiration because he repeated it several times."

"If you look for perfection, you'll never find it," Rosemary advised. "You haven't given up on men, have you? Not that you'll have a chance to meet anyone suitable where you're going."

How much closer could a person get than sharing living arrangements with a less than receptive guy who turned her knees to jelly? He'd done his best to discourage her. Not that she blamed him. No one in her right mind would be foolish enough to contemplate what was ahead of her, much less do it. Just thinking about him got her thoroughly confused. The pull to him was unmistakable, but completely impossible. He wanted her to fail. She couldn't afford to.

"I'm going away to learn something new, Rosemary, not husband shop." One of those was being provided.

"Pity. I can't imagine some silly old training program will be brimming over with excitement and exhilarating moments of passionate rapture."

The rapture was most likely going to be connected to getting through whatever Stephen Angelus had in mind to torture her with, Josie thought. She would have to take the dirt he dished out, proving to him, and to herself, she could overcome the odds.

"For all you know, the love of my life will be sitting next to me throughout the entire program."

Rosemary made a derisive sound in the back of her throat. "I must say you're going all out to impress him with your stylish wardrobe selections."

"The object is to be comfortable, not alluring," Josie reminded her.

"What's the heating pad for?" Rosemary asked.

"My back gets tired when I sit all day."

Something told her inactivity was the least of her worries. Concentrated heat was her best defense to relax sore muscles.

"And you're not going to tell me how long you'll be gone?" Rosemary would stop at nothing to pump for information.

"I honestly don't know, Rosemary. If I get through the initial phases, I may be chosen for the more intense stuff."

The first hurdle was getting through nothing more than a plane ride. Doing the Atlantic had been a piece of cake. Crossing the country would give her a good idea of what being with him day in and day out would be like.

"There isn't anything that says you have to stick with it, is there?" Rosemary tried again.

"Only my pride."

"I shouldn't have to remind you that's the first of the cardinal sins."

"Then don't, but I think pride is somewhere closer to the fourth one."

"Whatever." Rosemary waved a dismissive hand. "So, when you make it to the top of your class, what happens? Is the prize a one way ticket to Timbuktu?"

Josie giggled. "Nothing so grand as that, I'm afraid. Maybe a leaky boat ride through the Everglades."

"Oh, pet," Rosemary sighed, gathering Josie into a prodigious hug. "How can I let you go so quickly after I've just gotten you back? I don't care what you say, I'm going to the airport with you."

If Wendall had to tie her down, Rosemary was not allowed near the airport. She'd recognize Stephen immediately.

"I'll cry if you do, and I couldn't take the embarrassment."

"Then promise me you'll call the minute you get to Seattle," Rosemary pleaded.

"As soon as I can, I promise I'll call."

Wendell insisted they would have dinner at his club. Admonishing his wife that Josie had an early plane to catch, he refused to listen to any arguments. While it seemed reasonable he didn't have all of the pieces to fit together, he knew enough not to ask questions. As only he could, her godfather kept a steady stream of conversation going to keep Rosemary at bay.

Sleep, when it came, brought troubled dreams that constantly robbed Josie of rest. Now there was a new player and he was just as unsettling as the ghosts of her past, if not more so. They were behind her. He was ahead of her.

Since Rosemary was banned from going to the airport, she was not to be denied having Maxwell drive Josie there. Her godmother, who rarely stirred before noon, did enough crying for both of them, though it was a struggle not to join her.

"If you'd let the girl go, we might get to the airport on time," Maxwell observed glumly.

"Oh, hush up, Maxwell," Rosemary told him. "You've got plenty of time."

"The way you're carrying on," he said, "we may go down to the wire."

Reminding Josie to call her for a least the twenty-fifth time, Rosemary finally let her go. Waving her thoroughly wet handkerchief after the departing car, she watched Josie waving back until the bend in the drive obscured her from view.

"So, what'd you end up with? Talking gibberish or airplane parts?" Maxwell asked.

"Neither," she replied. "I'm taking over the CIA, but don't tell anybody. It's a surprise."

"Well hallelujah," he exclaimed. "Now I can rest easy at night. I thought maybe you were off to do something dangerous."

"Oh, no, nothing like that." *All I'm going to do is break my neck trying to please an ungrateful know-it-all who makes me want to rip my clothes off so he'll notice I'm a woman.* "I may run things over at the FBI too if I get bored."

"That ought to fix Miz Armature right up."

"You know how she is."

"Yep. That woman overreacts to everything."

"It's her nature, Maxwell. She can't help it."

"You know darn well she was all set to tell you how to run your life," he replied. "The last time you ran from her didn't work out so good. This time I got a feeling you're going to shine."

So much for Maxwell's predictive powers. Stephen Angelus was no Jason Giltner, but he was no cream puff either. Letting the companionable silence settle between them, Josie looked out at the rush hour traffic, glad to be absolved from the responsibility of driving in it. As jumpy as she was, she was better off not being behind the wheel. The airport loomed in front of her like some evil specter of doom, waiting to swallow her up in its unforgiving grip.

Thaddeus had been very precise when he called her about the flight. She was to check in alone under the name of Althea Hartmann. Normal security procedures to show identification would not be required. How that was going to work wasn't explained. Nor was she told where to meet Stephen. The lack of instructions suited her mood. Not knowing what to expect put her entirely at Stephen's mercy. That was probably part of his diabolical scheme to wear her down.

As Maxwell maneuvered the car as close to the entrance as he could get, she had a last minute urge to tell him she wanted to go back to Rosemary and Wendall. Standing off to the side, just inside the door, was the man she had no doubt was going to do his best to make her life a waking nightmare. Nothing could top what she'd already been through. Maybe, just maybe, she'd be so caught up in rivaling the daring Civil War spy, Bella Boyd, her memories would leave her alone.

"Here we are," Maxwell said in as cheerful a tone as his dour countenance would allow, offering his hand to help her from the car.

She wanted to hold on and not let go. A look of concern crossed his face.

"You gonna be all right, Josie?"

"Count on it, Maxwell," she answered, removing her hand from his. "I'll be back as soon as I have the entire work force snapped into shape. Give me the bags. I'm on my own from here on out."

Lifting the handles and tipping the suitcases onto their wheels, she gave her best imitation of a confident smile. As if he knew she was scared silly, Maxwell put a callused hand under her chin in a rare sign of affection.

"No one can hurt you so long as you don't let them get into your head," he told her softly. "Don't you forget that."

"I won't Maxwell." Her tears were a blink away. "Take care of yourself, okay?"

He took his hand away and touched it to his ever present cap. "Get going," he said gruffly. "I've got to move the car."

Realizing Stephen was watching the entire exchange, she started for the revolving door, ignoring him entirely, Once inside, she was forced to concede he was there.

"Let's go," he said without preamble, heading for the counter.

Like her, he had two bags. There was some small satisfaction that his were bigger than hers. At least he couldn't accuse her of having an unreasonable amount of luggage. Putting his cases on the scale, he made no move to help her with hers.

"Mr. and Mrs. Theodore Hartmann checking in," he said to the tired looking woman who greeted them. "I believe our tickets are being held for us."

Whatever magic it took to bypass the usual rigmarole, the forces were definitely in place. Putting both tickets and boarding passes in his shirt pocket, Stephen headed for the escalator. Dismissing the inclination to walk a respectful three paces behind, Josie lengthened her stride to walk beside him. Otherwise, she would have been forced to admire the curve of his rear end snugly encased in slim fitting jeans. The man might be rude, but he had great buns. As a matter of fact, she couldn't avoid admiring them when he forged ahead of her, taking a step above as the escalator moved upward. Apparently, his lessons as a devoted husband took a back seat to the other items on the agenda.

Fair enough. Two could play that game. Once she knew where their gate was, she veered away from him to go to the rest room. As apprehensive as she was about the days ahead, her fear of flying had first dibs on her bladder. In the confined privacy of the toilet stall, she did her best to practice a deep breathing exercise she had learned in an abortive attempt to master Yoga. The tears she had held back welled up of their own accord. She opened her purse in search of a tissue.

Stuffed in the center compartment of her handbag was a huge wad of bills she had most certainly not put there. Rosemary knew she would refuse. Quickly zipping the section closed, how much was there didn't matter. What would Stephen think of her carrying so much money? For that matter, what were the chances he'd be inspecting her personal effects when she wasn't around? Thaddeus had said every effort would be made to protect her privacy. Stephen Angelus hadn't said anything about his thoughts on that arrangement. Tears forgotten, her mind raced with possible hiding places before she realized how absurd that was. The time to face that was when they got where they were going. The more immediate impediment was presumably expecting her in the waiting area.

He was not only expecting her, he had clearly thought better of his initial approach and saved a seat for her. His neatly folded jacket marked the spot. As soon as he saw her coming toward him, he picked up his jacket and put it in his lap.

"I thought maybe you'd changed your mind," he said.

"That notion has occurred to me more than once," she admitted, "but necessity keeps pushing it away. When this is all behind us, if we're still speaking, we may have the good grace to agree neither of us got into the situation willingly."

"I have a lot of doubts," he said.

"So do I. Yours are probably much deeper than mine because you know the ropes."

"There are a few new wrinkles in this one than I've known before," he allowed. A hint of a smile showed at the corners of his mouth. "Aside from the obvious ones, that is."

"Which are?" she asked, settling into the seat next to him.

"I've always worked alone."

"By choice or by design?"

"Both actually."

A small, almost imperceptible tic showed briefly along the upper muscle of his right cheek. The motion told her she was treading on a sensitive subject. Either he didn't like talking about himself or preferred to leave the past assignments unmentioned. Either way, the message was clear. Stephen Angelus wasn't about to reveal anything personal unless he had no other choice. She could deal with that.

"If I'm reading you right," she said, subtly changing direction, "you're sort of feeling your way along with this just like I am. One thing's for sure. There isn't a pitfall you're concerned about that doesn't worry me too."

"You don't know what the pitfalls are."

"Oh, no? You described them perfectly without having to be specific. You think I'm not made of the stuff it takes to get the job done. That's because you don't know me. Let me tell you about myself. I'm a great believer in fair play. And you?"

Her question might fall on the short side of good sportsmanship. What did she have to lose? His eyes narrowed slightly as what she had asked registered. She knew the answer before he spoke.

"I deserved that," he said, shifting slightly in his seat. "Yes, I believe in a sense of fair play, but let me give you lesson number one. What you're about to get yourself into doesn't fit neatly into the protocol of human decency. The only rule is there are no rules. What your beliefs are has to take a back seat to making the mission successful. Would you like a cup of coffee?"

She got the picture. Any reaction on her part other than acceptance was a waste of time.

"Yes. Cream and sugar, please."

"Do you have anything you'd like to read?" he asked, not, she noticed, unkindly. "A magazine or something? I thought I'd get a paper."

"If they're out of survivalist magazines, I could make do with The New Yorker."

His smile acknowledged her insistence not to be cowed. "I'll see what I can do."

Watching him walk away, she examined the manner in which he carried himself. If it was possible to use incompatible terms, she had to categorize his demeanor as one of wary assurance. His gait was rhythmical, like that of a cat, sure footed and deliberate. He probably also knew how to move without making a sound, an asset for him, a possible disadvantage to her. The thought of him sneaking around without her being aware of it conjured up some sobering thoughts. The first thing she would check when they got to their final destination was the lock on her door.

During their training hours, she was at his disposal. On her own time, she felt certain a lot of personal regrouping would be required. The nagging thought she had done her best to pretend wasn't important was how attracted she was to a man bent on proving she couldn't make the grade. If he put a move on her and she responded, he'd use that against her. Not that he would do such a thing. Men like him, used to and secure in their own company, probably didn't need a woman in the same way other men did. What really disturbed her was wondering just what kind of lover Stephen Angelus was.

Considering that side of him was still very much on her mind as he came back into view. Fortunately he wasn't close enough to hear her sharp intake of breath in reaction to the open appraisal she was getting from him. Her breasts hardened in direct response to the caress of his gaze and she self-consciously pulled her parka closed to cover them.

"Are you cold?" he asked, handing a steaming cup of coffee to her.

She shook her head, smothering the inclination to let him know she had caught his fleeting lapse of behavior. Maybe he had meant it as a warning. To be on the safe side, she'd take it as such.

"Tell me about the place where we're going," she said, anxious to get on neutral ground. "I don't mean the rain and the skeighty-eight million trees. I mean the place where we will be staying."

"It's a house." Having given her that all-encompassing description, he took a sip of coffee.

"Boy, that sure tells me a lot," she said. "I can picture it exactly. A house."

"Thaddeus refers to it as a cabin because it's in the woods, I think. As far as I'm concerned, it's a house. Two stories. Kitchen, living room, dining room. Bedrooms upstairs."

"With bathrooms thrown in for that homey touch, I hope," she said.

"Both bedrooms have their own and there's a john downstairs next to the utility room with a washer and dryer," he elaborated.

"That answers the laundry question. Where do we go for food and other stuff we need?"

"There's a grocery store in Boulder Creek," he told her. "The place will be stocked with everything we need when we get there."

"Thaddeus thinks of everything, doesn't he?"

Stephen frowned. Either he didn't like the question or didn't know how he wanted to answer it. He finally half shrugged and started reading the paper he had brought with the coffee. If she accepted his bad manners at the onset, she'd be forced to keep doing it. Screw that.

"I guess they were all out of the New Yorker," she reminded him.

"Huh? I forgot to look."

"Then share the paper unless you've figured out how to read all of the sections simultaneously."

He handed her the sports. It figured. She helped herself to the business section, putting the sports back on his lap. He didn't look at her, but that muscle in his cheek was twitching again. Evidently he had made all of the effort he was going to make. Still, she got the distinct feeling he was holding back something he wanted to say.

Putting her paper aside, she looked over at him. It came as no surprise he was now staring at her. As close as she was, every finely chiseled feature of him reached out to touch her. In spite of herself, she examined his lips, imagining how he would kiss her. Neither of them moved, locked in a battle of wills not to be the first to look away. Josie won. After all, she had more to lose than he did.

"That's going to be a problem," he said with a ragged edge to his voice she had not heard before.

"What," she asked feigning innocence.

"I'm not in the habit of spouting purple prose," he said, letting his eyes linger on her lips until she had all she could do to keep from squirming. "There are a lot of reasons this caper doesn't appeal to me, not the least of which is how you seem to be able to make my mind wander where it shouldn't be. I'm not blaming you. It's quite candidly the way things are. I will do my job because I have to go where I am sent, but nothing in the rule book says I have to socialize with you."

"You've done a great job of avoiding that so far," she told him, struggling to keep her breathing even. "However, I don't see how we can escape some contact in order for me to learn what I have to know. Since you've set the stage that it's okay to be frank, I'll follow suit." She took a deep breath. "Regardless of how I affect you or you affect me, we're not going to help things by seeing which one of us can snarl the most. Go right ahead and play the brooding loner. I don't care. When the time comes to convince a certain party how happy we are together, you'll be the one to blow it, not I."

There. She had said it. From the looks of him, she had hit home. He wasn't just mad. He was livid.

"Don't ever presume to question my ability," he snapped, not bothering to mask his anger.

"Why not?" she snapped back. "You've had a field day making an issue of mine. The way I look at it, we have two ways to go. We can be civil or we can be contemptuous. I don't see the second option being to our advantage, do you?"

A flood of emotions played across his face. He had not been prepared for her burst of temper any more than she had. Such eruptions were rare. Stephen Angelus had put his finger on her ego and pushed too hard. Maybe he thought she wasn't the type to fight back. Now he knew differently.

What he did next was so natural, she didn't have time to react. Leaning toward her, his hand went behind her neck to draw her face to his. The ascent of his mouth on hers happened too fast for her to make even a feeble stab of pretending to avoid him. As soon as their lips met, she senses were much too occupied to make any attempt at indifference. Kissing Stephen Angelus, she quickly discovered, was the purest form of pleasure. Answering each inquisitive move he made to extend the contact convinced her she wanted more. When he broke away, she could still feel the tingling sensation of him.

"I'll make my best attempt to be civil," he said, his face still only inches from hers. "What you have to understand is by nature I am a solitary man. If I stay away from you it's because I know the dangers of getting too close."

The pounding of her heart filled her ears. She had envisioned hard and brutal. She had gotten soothing and skillful. Unlike him, she craved companionship. Until now. Any further contact between them was too chancy. In mere seconds he had proved how easy it was for her to lose her perspective.

"You're absolutely right," she said, amazed by her reaction to the warmth of his breath on her face. "Civil and separate it is."

His eyes searched hers, looking, she thought, for some sign of insincerity. She knew very well the aftermath of his kiss was written all over her face. Taking his hand from the back of her head, he trailed a finger down her cheek, smiling at her response.

"Now you know why marriages are made in heaven," he said. "Thaddeus Muldoon has a lot to learn."

As far as she was concerned, Thaddeus Muldoon had made a clever match. His only flaw was forgetting to tell her where pretend ended and real began. Then it struck her. Stephen Angelus knew. It was up to her to figure it out for herself.

Chapter Five

❖

The place hadn't changed. Thaddeus liked the facility because of its remote location. His argument was that the chances of anyone being interested in the occasional activity at the site were non-existent. There simply was nobody within range to notice. The thick woods were made to order for tramping through on endurance building treks that at one time had been a staple of the training routine. Now those same routes he had traveled so often would be used for only one purpose. To convince Josie Giltner to get the hell out of his life.

It that didn't work, he had other plans at his disposal, such as what he told her to do immediately when they entered the house. Thaddeus had given her credit for extremely sharp observation skills. The time was ripe for her to prove it. His instructions to her were brief. Look over the house from top to bottom. In one hour be prepared to provide him with a complete description of each room. From memory. No note taking.

He knew he was being unfair, but fairness didn't figure into getting rid of her. She was tired. So much the better. He was tired too. Assignments never adhered to catching a person at his best. Every schedule took on a life of its own. She needed to realize that.

"Time's up," he called out to her, not sure where she was.

In an instant, she appeared around the staircase that divided the living room and dining room. Instead of the frazzled woman he was hoping for, she wore the calm composure of a nun on her way to evening prayers.

"Where shall I start?" she asked.

"Anywhere you like," he replied, going into the living room and sitting down.

She followed him, but remained standing. Her pose reminded him of someone poised to present prepared remarks. No speaker he had ever seen looked quite so mouth-watering in faded jeans that encased her long, slender legs and a casual sweater that accented the swell of her breasts. The kiss had been an idiotic mistake. His concentration was centered on the taste of her now, along with the enticing visual picture standing in front of him.

"All of the furnishings in the house are of inferior quality. Government issue most likely," she began. He hadn't even noticed the furnishings. "Everything is designed to be utilitarian without any consideration for comfort."

"It's a training facility," he reminded her, "not a four star hotel."

She heard him of course. What she didn't do was react to him, continuing her monologue as if he hadn't said a word.

"Although similar in size, the bedroom where you will be staying is slightly larger than the one you said I should take. About an extra square foot would be my guess. The décor of both rooms is a hodgepodge of styles and colors, most of which don't match."

Launching into a brief description of the various pieces in each room, nothing was left out, including sloppy housekeeping touches. He found it surprising she hadn't included a dust bunny count. Stopping her was an option. She had proved her competence to note her surroundings easily. Her overview was so complete she had even noticed the FAX machine located in his bedroom was out of paper. Not letting her finish would be an admission he had been wrong about her. So she was good at detail. So what? No. That wasn't right. The woman was a master of detail, rounding out her account by listing a brief report of cabinet contents in the kitchen.

"You didn't tell me how precise I was to be," she finished up, "but I feel I've presented an accurate picture."

"It will do."

Under no circumstances would she receive any praise from him. In the first place, he never praised his trainees. In the second place, she was bound to take any encouragement as an endorsement. The fact he had never kissed any of his trainees either had no bearing on the matter whatsoever.

"Is that all for now?" she asked, "or do you have something else in mind?"

He had something else in mind all right. "You've had a long day," he conceded. "We'll take this up in the morning."

"At what time?"

"Just be ready, he answered, vaguely on purpose.

She had no call to look at him the way she did with her eyes so full of questions. Up close they were definitely twin magnets of promises to come. From a distance, they could drive him just as wild. The proof of that was inclined to rise in swollen anticipation of forbidden relief he didn't dare consider.

"I'm going to make a cup of tea," she informed him, "and then I think I'll turn in."

"None for me," he said, taking for granted he would be included.

"I didn't offer you any," she reminded him as she left the room.

He should correct the presumption. His inference was boorish at best. So be it. The front was his best line of defense. By tomorrow night, Josie Giltner would be ready to pack it in. He'd see to that. She might be a whiz at interior design. It was a safe bet a close inspection of the local flora and fauna would prove to be her undoing.

Turning on the television to fill the silence, he doggedly stayed where he was in a show of total disinterest. A keen sense of hearing followed her of its own accord. He guessed she took the tea upstairs with her because he could hear movement in the room above. Then the water pipes sprang into action. A bath or a shower? He couldn't tell. For either pursuit, she would need to bare that lithe body he ached to feel beneath his own. Rather than punish himself further, he put out the lights and went upstairs himself.

All of the usual ploys he used to get his mind to click off met with limited success. The problem was not so much getting himself to relax as it was his preoccupation with being sure he got up at the ungodly hour he had planned to roust her from her warm blankets into the damp chill of early morning. Try to outfox him, would she? After traipsing around in the woods all day, she'd run screaming for the creature comforts of civilization. As he dragged himself out of bed at four in the morning, the thought occurred to him that in an effort to penalize her, he was in reality hurting himself.

Dressed for the challenge ahead, he opened his bedroom door. Damn if he didn't smell coffee. His shrinking violet was proving herself to be one bona fide frustrating female. She was sitting at the kitchen table cupping a mug of coffee in both hands.

"I can fix my own coffee," he said sourly, noticing she had put a cup on the counter for him.

"Suit yourself," she replied. "Making two pots seems kind of dumb to me."

"What I mean is," he back pedaled, "you aren't expected to handle the kitchen duties. I'll fix my own meals. I prefer to eat alone."

"That's your prerogative, but I don't mind playing this part of the sham for real. Not every wife gets her jollies out of cooking. I happen to like it. If you change your mind, let me know."

"I won't."

Going to the hall closet, he took out two backpacks he had asked to have outfitted and left for them. Hers was the same weight as his, guaranteed to whittle her down in no time.

"Here." he said, putting hers on the floor at her feet. "You'll be needing this."

Lifting it cautiously, she put the pack on the table. "How long are we going to be gone?" she asked.

"Until you wear out," he answered. "I'll bring you back here tonight." Carry her was more like it.

To his surprise, she opened the pack to inspect its contents. He had not counted on that. Meek acceptance was not to be. The table quickly filled with items a one day hike did not require.

"What are you doing" he demanded. Why did she have to be so damn clever?

"When our trek across Siberia enters into the picture, I'm sure some of this stuff will come in handy," she explained, showing a patience that aggravated him more than he already was. "For today, I think these things are overkill. If you like lugging around extra weight, that's your choice."

"You need to be prepared in the event of every emergency. Put that stuff back," he ordered.

"Look," she said, facing him squarely. "You're the expert and I respect that. Assigning me a man's backpack no doubt appeals to your twisted sense of humor. I am not amused."

"This is not a source of amusement," he said sternly, starting to react to those unbelievable violet eyes.

"A matter of life and death I believe was how you put it. I'll buy that, but let's see what it takes to break the little lady is just plain childish. There," she said, pulling the zipper closed firmly, "this I can handle. When do we start?"

"In five minutes."

She was made of sterner stuff than he was willing to admit. All he needed to do was exhaust her. Thaddeus would kill him if he purposefully mistreated her and she complained about it. Looking out of the kitchen window, he saw he had an ally after all. It was raining.

Sloshing up one hill and down the next. he kept up a pace meant to achieve his purpose. Josie plodded along with unflappable determination he was sure would wane before long. Not once did she ask to stop or fall behind. As he was prone to do, he emptied his mind and eventually forgot she was there. He had learned the technique as a means of survival. In time, he found he depended on the exercise to keep his sanity. Coming to a level area, he selected a rock to sit on and reached into his pack for a bottle of water. Wordlessly, she did the same.

Guardedly scrutinizing her for signs of fatigue, he saw none. The woman who had worn her feelings so openly had taken on the look of a sphinx. Dampness created a fringe of tiny curls around her face, giving a whimsical look to her fragile beauty. He looked away, focusing instead on the awesome view the clearing provided. When she moved, he turned back to see her disappearing into the trees.

"Where are you going?" he demanded.

"To commune with nature in private," she answered, continuing on her way, "unless that's part of the observation process."

As the day progressed, her stoicism remained in place. Allowing time for them to eat, his disposition was not improved by the prepackaged fare he choked down. What rankled him was Josie had eliminated most of her supply of bland high protein issue, replacing it with food she had prepared herself. How long she had been up and working in the kitchen before he got out of bed didn't matter. Her lack of sleep could only work to his advantage.

By midafternoon, his energy was fading and the raw edge of his nerves was close to its peak. Now was the time for the coup de grace.

"That's enough for today," he announced magnanimously. Then he dropped his bomb. "You get us back to base."

The flash of disgust in her eyes was brief. He caught it nonetheless. Finally he could bask in the shining brilliance of success. She'd have to ask for help and he'd refuse. Spending a night in the unforgiving arms of nature was not something he looked forward to, but the end justified the means if that's what it took. His victim looked up at the sky as if searching for divine guidance. The rain had turned to a fine mist and the chances were good she was soaked through to the skin.

Adjusting her backpack, she started walking. Before they had gone very far, he realized she was leading them directly back to the house, retracing his route almost step by step. He could clearly hear the resounding pop as his bubble burst. As hard as it was to concede defeat, he had no other choice. His hostility was slowing changing to grudging respect. Not that he planned to go down without a fight. His stockpile of ammunition wasn't depleted yet.

Not a word passed between them until they reached the house. As they went through the front door, she finally said something.

"Am I in for the same tomorrow or have you proved your point?"

She was pissed. He didn't blame her.

"We have just begun your discipline." he told her. "It may not make much sense to you, but mental toughness is worthless without physical endurance. The best advice I can give you is to expect the unexpected. That's what this job is all about."

"Is that a yes?" she asked.

"Today was the introductory phase, a level one experience if you will." He was beginning to gather steam again. "Until you make it through the entire series, you aren't considered qualified to function in the field."

"Fine. That's tomorrow. What about now? Am I on my own until morning?"

"If you need to rest, just say so," he baited her.

"What I need is to get out of these clothes and so do you." If looks could have killed, he'd be a goner. "Or is wearing wet clothing indefinitely part of the discipline?" Her accent on the last word sharply conveyed her opinion of the program he was administering.

"May I suggest you get rid of the nine to five mentality?" he challenged her.

"So far, I'm in a five to four-thirty frame of mind," she retorted. "This is supposed to be a training program, not a full scale operation to bring Communist China to its knees. I'll be glad to go with the flow if you'll be good enough to tell me what the flow is."

"Change your clothes," he directed, desperately trying not to envision how she would look while she did. "We've both put in a full day."

It was a small concession, but she had earned it. Considering herself dismissed, she took off up the stairs. Ridding himself of his backpack, he hauled his weary bones into a hot shower. What he wouldn't do for a thick steak smothered in onions and a bottle of good wine. Such luxuries were not included. His skill at keeping most microwave entrees from turning to rubber had reached a reasonable level of competence and would have to do.

The shower helped. So did the odorless liniment he'd brought along to ease the effects of stain. If Josie wasn't thoroughly exhausted, she should be. He was. Certain occupational hazards were necessary. His muscles could stand the toning. There would be plenty of time to rest while Thaddeus beat the bushes finding a more suitable wife for him. Gathering up his wet clothes, he headed down the stairs to deposit his load in the dryer,

His senses were immediately assaulted by a wave of inviting odors that set off a furious rumble in his stomach. The greatest equalizer was hunger. That he knew. She couldn't have chosen a better infliction of pain in retaliation for his treatment of her. Regret for having boasted of his ability to handle his own cooking needs instantly reared its ugly little head and stuck its tongue out at him. Sometimes he was too damn cocky for his own good.

If he wanted dry clothes, he had to go through the kitchen. Assuming an air of indifference, he stepped into the room.

"I thought maybe you had drowned," she said, checking a pot on the stove and replacing the lid. "As soon as you put those things in the dryer, sit down and eat."

Angels, he had been told, come in all shapes and sizes. The apparition in slacks and a sweatshirt wielding a spoon may not have been heaven sent, but she was far and away the best he had ever seen.

"I said I'd take care of myself," he protested without much conviction.

"Shut up and eat," she commanded. "We're into my area of expertise now and I'm in no mood for any of your lip."

Her face was flushed from the heat of the stove. Those eyes that mesmerized him dared him to refuse. He did exactly as he was told.

"For tonight only," he cautioned, taking a large helping of everything offered to him.

"Oh, quit blustering," she chastised. "It's not only tiresome, it's unbecoming. I'll adhere to your grinding attempt to break my spirit, but when it comes to the kitchen, you're in my domain."

"I'm not entirely ignorant of the various functions," he informed her, knowing full well he couldn't have produced a meal of the caliber he was eating if his life depended on it.

"That's good to know," she said sweetly. "I was beginning to think you were very one dimensional."

"I take my work seriously," he defended himself. "That's part of my nature."

"What's another part of your nature?"

"What difference does it make?" He was immediately suspicious.

"I'd like to know."

"Maybe it's better you don't. This is a business that doesn't adhere to a general office routine."

"How would you know?" she asked. "Have you ever worked in an office?"

"No.'

"So this is the only job you've ever had?"

"Yes."

"I see. I guess that's why you seem so out of touch. It makes sense when I think about it. Everything you believe in or feel has to be repressed in order to function as whomever you're supposed to be."

She wasn't being sarcastic or critical. If anything, she was being genuinely sympathetic.

"Ideally, that's what you try to achieve," he agreed. "Sometimes it's easier than others."

"Such as when you think the person with whom you're being forced to work doesn't measure up to the standard?"

"I told you it wasn't personal." Why, all of a sudden, did it make any difference to him what she thought? "Under other circumstances, I'd probably enjoy getting to know you."

"Really?"

Now she was skeptical. With good reason.

"You sacrifice a lot when you do what I do," he explained. "It's hard to combine a successful private life with a professional one. You always end up sacrificing one for the other."

"Sounds like the perfect place for widows and orphans," she observed. "Are you either one of those?"

"No."

"Well, I fit both categories and you'd be surprised how adaptable those experiences make you. What was it about this kind of work that appealed so much to you?"

As strange as it was, no one had ever asked him that. The answer slipped out before he could stop it.

"I wanted to get away from being pressured into something I wasn't inclined to do. To be honest, I wasn't really fully aware of what I was getting myself into."

"But you found you liked it?" she asked.

"I adjusted." She didn't need to know he had been miserable. "The atmosphere was not the same as it is now."

"Was Thaddeus there?"

"Thaddeus has been around so long he witnessed the dawn of time. No organization has a fixture more firmly entrenched than he."

"Is that a statement of admiration or toleration?"

"Both. The man is probably the most brilliant tactician in the world today. Because I respect him doesn't mean I have to like him."

"Do you like him?"

"It's hard not to."

"Dumping me in your lap must have put a strain on that."

"You can like someone without always agreeing with them."

"How true. I'm not the problem, am I, Stephen?"

She had never said his name. He should correct her and remind her they were Theodore and Althea. The way she was looking at him with her head resting on her hands made it impossible. He wanted to get closer to her, not farther away.

"In some ways you are and in some ways you aren't," he admitted.

"This assignment is far removed from what you have been doing, isn't it?"

"I'd say that a fair assessment."

"Do women in general bother you or is it just me?"

"Were you always so subtle or is it an acquired art?"

She laughed, a rich, full-bodied sound that he couldn't help but join. Then she was serious again.

"I'd really like to know."

What was the harm in telling her? She was very persistent.

"My opinion of women, like most of my other opinions, is skewed by unfamiliarity as much as anything else. I've only known one woman I truly admired and she has been dead for a long time."

"Your mother."

"How did you know?" Had Thaddeus been babbling behind his back?

"I didn't know. I guessed."

"Oh. What else have you guessed?"

"Do you really want to know?"

"Yes." As long as she looked at him the way she was, she could do anything she damn well pleased.

"Some of the things you say, along with your accent, remind me of the chauvinistic mentality of the old South."

He started to bristle. She held up her hand.

"That's not a put-down. It's a situation I think you were born into. You and a lot of others. The scenario usually includes a domineering, opinionated patriarch who has the good luck to marry a woman of breeding. That doesn't stop him from espousing male superiority to his sons. In his mind, a woman belongs at home to do his bidding. Any woman who does otherwise is either a whore or a lesbian."

Having just described Andrew Angelus perfectly, Josie sat back in her chair. Stephen wondered idly how she had become such an expert on men like his father.

"Then does it follow that the sons are raised in the image of their sires?" he asked.

"Sometimes. That's how the myth gets perpetrated. I don't think you stayed around long enough to get the whole shebang."

She was right. He hadn't.

"What did I do?" he asked.

"You already told me. When your father was ready to mold you as he saw fit, you got out and joined the foreign legion."

"You're quite perceptive," he observed.

"Not really. Call it overexposure. I used to amuse myself trying to figure people out. It helped pass the time."

He suspected there was more to it than that. The woman who had hiked in the woods all day and then prepared an enticing dinner to boot was a mass of contradictions. It was only natural he should be intrigued. Not only was she beautiful and alluring, she was also totally unpredictable. That was a bewitching combination, tempting him to go beyond the boundaries of permissible standards. Still unconvinced she could make the grade, there was no harm in getting some pleasure out of one of the few mistakes Thaddeus had ever made.

"What's it like to be married?" he asked Josie.

Her double take proved she could be caught off guard. The question had popped into his mind all of a sudden. Why, he had no idea.

"I'm not sure my marriage qualifies me to give you a very good answer," she said, measuring every word.

"I shouldn't have asked."

"No, it's a reasonable question. Before the bottom fell out, I thought we had everything the way it should be. Of course, aside from what happened, I don't think we were all that typical."

"What do you mean?" He discovered he really wanted to know.

"The majority of my friends who are married sort of went by a pattern. After the wedding and honeymoon, they settled in. A few bought a house. Most started with an apartment. He worked. She worked. Usually long hours. Togetherness was pretty much a catch as catch can situation. Social life revolved around his buddies and her girlfriends. The bliss part never quite got the attention it deserved. They weren't unhappy necessarily. They were just working out the new arrangement."

"It sounds dreary."

"Doesn't it? Like it or not, that's how most marriages are, I think."

"And yours wasn't?"

"Not really. Our marriage was more like one big party interspersed with weekends in the country to get away from it all. The spiral just kept going until it blew up. Now, I know why. At the time I thought the quiet moments and learning about each other had to be sacrificed for the mad pace we kept. Looking back, I'm chagrined at my stupidity."

"We've all done things that are hard to explain."

"It's nice of you to include yourself. I can't imagine you falling for the line I did."

"I didn't get married, but I fell for the line."

He hadn't thought about Vivian in years. There had been a time when he thought of nothing but her. Sharing that with Josie was the last thing he had on his mind. He had never shared Vivian with anyone. He wasn't about to start now.

Josie smiled at him. "For such a grouch, you do have a nice side to you. If you're finished, I think I'll clean up and turn in."

"Great meal," he told her, pushing his chair back. "You go on. I'll clean up."

"Are you sure?"

"Those are the functions I know that I was telling you about earlier."

Her smile reached inside of him to a defenseless place no one was allowed to touch. Confused by his reaction, he sought the familiar comfort of pretending he couldn't care less. She didn't stick around to watch him struggle with long-suppressed yearnings he was convinced he could control. Although she had left the room, her presence was still with him. He had to break her. Otherwise the wanting would consume him.

Only the deeply ingrained habit of protecting his butt kept him from going after her. What he wanted had nothing to do with pushing a determined woman beyond the limits of her endurance to prove she couldn't keep up with him. The type of surrender he'd much rather have was coaxing her body to move with his until they both were lost to everything except each other. There weren't many women who could do that to a man. He knew without reservation Josie was more than capable.

That made her dangerous from every angle. Not dangerous like Vivian had been in her cold, calculated attempt to carve out a healthy chunk of Angelus money before moving on to her next conquest. The risk Josie posed was too elusive to be measured by a yardstick. She would capture much more than a fortune, leaving him helpless to keep up the resolve that was the solid protection he depended on to keep himself apart. His only defense was to pile on the pressure.

No more dinners together and no more conversations to throw him off balance. Theirs was a relationship going nowhere. The last thing he needed was to feel guilty because he caused her defeat. If all else failed, he'd climax her demise with a brisk march up Bataan Ridge.

Named by a colleague, the ridge was a treacherous obstacle course nature had created that Stephen had discovered. Taking Josie there would be a last resort. There was no way he could justify quite yet putting her through an ordeal few men could complete successfully.

Desperation was a stern task master. Thaddeus could damn well find him a wife from among the corps, preferably a horsey bitch with the sex appeal of a fire hydrant. He couldn't handle soft curves and tempting lips. His path was set. Nothing in the plan included quixotic notions, carnal or otherwise.

It rained all night. Hauling himself out of bed at three in the morning to the painful accompaniment of protesting muscles, he reminded himself repeatedly it was the result, not the method that mattered. Instead of pounding on her door as he should have, he pushed it open and turned on the glaring overhead light. His course charted, he strode to the bed before he lost his nerve, throwing back the covers with a flourish.

"Rise and shine," he barked out in his best drill sergeant tone.

Well-bred women, he had always supposed, wore long nightgowns or sensible pajamas to bed. Josie Giltner wore neither. She was stark naked. Unprepared for what he was seeing, his body instantly responded to the lush fullness of her breasts reacting to the sudden blast of cold air. Twin pink centers puckered quickly into tantalizing peaks as her eyes flew open.

"Is it time to get up?" she asked, showing no reaction to his gaping admiration of the scene in front of him. He managed a weak nod. "Then I'd better head for the shower," she informed him.

Giving every appearance of finding the situation completely normal, she slid across the bed in the direction of the bathroom. Still in a trance, he stared dumbly at the door she closed firmly behind her. His initial burst of desire had blossomed into a full blown erection struggling to free itself from the confines of his pants. In total confusion, he grappled with gaining even the slightest measure of composure. A rational man would have had the good sense to admit she outclassed him. In his current condition, clear thinking did not come easily. His new attack approach was not going as well as he had hoped.

Nor did things improve as the week wore on. If anything, Josie grew stronger. His patience, never one of his superior attributes to begin with, was wearing thinner by the minute. To make matters worse, his desire for her ran wild regardless of how tired he was. The more he wanted to rid himself of her, the more he wanted her. Whatever resources she was drawing on showed no sign of drying up. Rather than concede he had underestimated her, he steadfastly stuck to his routine. The time had come for Bataan Ridge.

"We have a new challenge today," he informed her, relishing the sweet taste of victory he knew was coming.

"Don't tell me," she replied, echoing his false bravado with maddening precision. "You've decided to enter us in the Ironman competition. If it's all the same to you, I'll pass."

"Is that an admission you can't keep up?" he asked hopefully.

"As much as you'd like to hear I'm bowing out, don't hold your breath." Her chin rose in a pose of defiance he had seen with regularity as the days passed. "You lead. I'll follow. That's how you like things to work, isn't it?"

"Do I denote a tinge of bitterness in your voice?" he asked her.

"Let me assure you I have no intention of hiding how I feel," she retorted. "I'm more than willing to bow to your expertise, but heavy-handed masochism seems extreme, even for you. If you only heard a tinge of bitterness in my voice, you weren't listening."

She was crumbling. He could sense it. Her body might be holding up admirably. The mental strain combined with a lack of sleep was finally having an effect.

"That's always the problem with green recruits," he shot back at her, pressing what he thought was an advantage. "They always think things should be made easier just for them."

"And you're just the guy to bring them to their knees, aren't you? Well, my knees are perfectly fine, thank you very much, so let's get this new challenge out of the way, shall we?"

Without giving him a chance to reply, she was out of the door, splashing into the rain. By now, the ground was thoroughly saturated, turning the paths into a slippery hazard of mud that clung to their boots making walking difficult. It was a perfect day for sitting in front of a crackling fire slowly exploring long, slender legs and a body created to entice. Damn his thoughts. In a matter of hours, he could put Josie Giltner out of his mind forever. Quickly overtaking his prey, he led her toward her Waterloo.

On a clear sunlit day, Bataan Ridge was about as inviting as a pit of cobras ready to strike. In the driving rain, there was no mistaking the menacing aspects of the dangerous uphill grade looming in front of them.

"Well, here we are," he announced grandly, waving his hand over the vista awaiting them. "This is where we separate the men from the boys."

Looking at her would have forced him to reconsider. Better to just keep going until she begged him to stop. He thought he heard her say something, but the howling wind swallowed voices along with the guilt he tried so hard to hide. After the first mile, the incline steepened sharply. Maintaining a stable foothold took all of his strength. Sure Josie would find the course impossible, he plodded upward, waiting to hear a call for a halt that never came. Finally pausing for breath, he looked behind him.

No one was there.

She must have found the going tougher than he thought. Retracing his steps, he made his way carefully down the slippery slope. Josie was nowhere to be seen. The icy clutch of panic didn't set in immediately. His obstinacy wouldn't let it. She's fine, he kept telling himself, going faster to satisfy the fading hope she would come into view at any minute. She didn't. My God, she's hurt took over with a vengeance, turning his stomach into knots as he fought the image of Josie lying bleeding in some deep ravine made impassable by the weather,

If he was honest, the course was in no shape for even the best qualified to be attempting it. Why couldn't he have left well enough alone? If she was hurt, he'd never forgive himself. When would he learn to face facts and accept the inevitable? Why did he insist on having his own way no matter what?

"Just be alive, Josie," he muttered to himself, hardly aware he was speaking out loud. "I promise no more endurance tests. You've passed. You win. I give in."

No one answered. Not even the wind. An eerie silence had settled over the mountains, much like the deadly calm in the eye of a hurricane. At a point far above the valley where the house was located, he could see most of the path leading downward. The path was empty. Adjusting his binoculars, he scanned the area in front of the house. Everything looked the same as always. Except something seemed to be missing. It took him a few minutes to figure it out.

The car was gone.

Chapter Six

❖

Somehow the simple act of pushing a grocery cart up and down aisles calmed her. Lord knows, she needed something to remind her there was a normal world still limping along without being jerked around by Stephen Angelus. How dare he pull such a stunt? A new challenge indeed. He had deliberately chosen an exercise he knew she couldn't do no matter what shape she was in. Did he really want her to kill herself? Or would a simple maiming do?

Day after day he ran the gamut of his own brand of psychological warfare, now and then remembering to be human. Occasionally, he dropped the brusque mannerisms. Then, giving no warning, he was cold and withdrawn again as if she had some rare disease he didn't want to catch. Underneath it all, she suspected his motives were purely self-centered. His world had been torn apart and he didn't like it. What a shame. Did he think she'd been riding the gravy train?

Maybe that was being unfair. There was so much about him she didn't know. After all, she had walked into the lion's den driven entirely by necessity. Taking time to collect details hadn't been an option offered. It stood to reason he hadn't been given much in the way of choices either. Thrown together with a total novice, he had fought back in the only way he knew. Separate the men from the boys, would he? How about doing everything in his power to rid himself of her?

He thought he had won, but he hadn't. No one could fault her for telling him to take a flying leap. As usual, he forged ahead, assuming she was blindly following behind, impervious to his special brand of torture. Like their first day's hike. Did he really think she was so dumb she wouldn't notice the markings on trees that designated the route he had laid out for them? No one had a better supply of zingers than he did. Whenever she showed signs of stumbling, he was right there to offer a discouraging word. What did it take to please the man?

Food wasn't the answer. Although he obviously distained eating with her, that didn't stop him from stuffing himself every night. Then, he had the gall to keep getting her up before dawn to be sure she dragged herself through his so-called discipline. As hard as it was, she hadn't complained. Every inch of her hurt, but he didn't know that. Nor would he. So he thought she would pack her bags, did he? Well, he could think again.

Looking down at her cart, Josie realized she had put nothing in it. The list in her hand had gone unnoticed as her mind raced through the indignity she had forced herself to accept. Let Stephen Angelus play out his sorry little game. She had groceries to buy. It would serve him right if she started lacing his food with arsenic, if she could find some. Under no circumstances would she allow her brave front to crumble.

"Mrs. Hartmann?"

Something clicked inside of her as she glanced up at the strange man addressing her. She was supposed to be Mrs. Hartmann. Had Stephen devised another test to trap her into blowing the whole deal? Not likely. Stephen didn't know where she was.

"Yes?" she said, doing her best to sound pleasant.

"I thought that was you. I'm Joseph Cooper. I live in the brown shingled house you pass on the way up to yours."

Joseph Cooper had the look of a crusty backwoodsman who fended for himself in spite of his advanced years. How did he know the Hartmann name? Now what was she supposed to do? Her only choice was to wing it, saying as little as possible.

"Is that the house with the white shutters?" she asked.

"You've got it. I hope you don't think I'm too forward. Normally I wouldn't bother you, but when disaster measures are being put into place, I can't stand idly by," Joseph Cooper informed her.

"Of course not." What disaster?

"I was going to come up to your house, but when I saw you heading for town, I figured you were laying in supplies. Most people don't think of that. They figure they don't need to bother, I guess. We locals aren't quite so blasé. We've been through too many of these things to take them lightly."

What was he talking about? There had to be some way she could find out without letting him know she didn't have the foggiest idea what he was trying to tell her.

"How lucky we are to have you for a neighbor."

"I don't know about that, but I'm glad to share the wealth of my experience. With any luck, the rain will stop. If it doesn't, you should know the procedures. You wouldn't want to be stuck in your house with no electricity and no way out."

So that was it. "Does that happen often?"

"A few years back, the flooding was terrible. Washed the road clean away, it did. The ground around here can only take so much, you know. Now, mind you, if the situation gets anywhere near serious, you'll be encouraged to evacuate."

"Encouraged?"

"Well, when it's in the interest of public safety, there's not much of a choice. Getting buried by a mud slide or being crushed by a falling tree wouldn't be a pleasant was to go."

"Heavens no. Forgive me for asking, but how did you find out my name?" Something told her Stephen would have a conniption fit if he knew anyone might know who they were.

"I just asked Flora over at the real estate office. She can get the name of any property owner from that computer of hers."

Apparently pleased with his ingenuity, Joseph showed no sign of concern he might be compromising Flora's access to what might well be confidential information. Josie didn't know if it was or not. What amazed her was how well the groundwork had been laid to establish a credible cover for her and Stephen.

"Flora sounds like a handy lady to know," she observed.

"She's my sister-in-law," he said with a grin. "I've got pull. Anyway, what I was going to check with you about was they're asking for standby volunteers over at the fire company to help fill sandbags."

"I couldn't do that without speaking to my husband."

"You look kind of puny to be doing such work if you don't mind me saying so. I thought maybe your husband would lend a hand."

So she looked puny, did she? Wouldn't Joseph be surprised to know how she had spent the past eight days"

"I'll be sure to ask him," she assured Joseph.

"If I had your phone number, I could give you a call when he'd be needed."

Something told her to avoid that one. As resourceful as Flora was, access to unlisted phone numbers evidently was not included in her bag of tricks.

"I feel terrible, Mr. Cooper," Josie feigned genuine dismay, "but I haven't learned the number yet."

"That's okay." Joseph bought her excuse without blinking an eye. "I'll just knock on your door if it comes to that."

Wouldn't Stephen be thrilled? Somehow he didn't strike her as the pitch in and help type.

"I hate to put you to so much trouble."

"No trouble at all," Joseph assured her. "I'll catch you later. I want to be sure I'm up-to-date on my TV programs in case we have to evacuate."

Twirling his cart around, Joseph took off in the direction of the check-out counters. The brief brush with civilized conversation had a rejuvenating jolt to it after over a week of Stephen's company. Gathering her wits together, Josie started searching for the items on her list. That would probably meet with Stephen's disapproval too. The only time her bogus husband had shown a sustained human response was that morning he'd frozen her out of a nice warm bed.

Okay. Her thoughts had strayed where they didn't belong. What was it about him she found so irresistible in spite of his undisguised contempt for her? As much as she had questioned her instincts since Jason's death, one aspect had remained intact. She could still figure out when a man was on the make. When Stephen thought they had said good-bye at the airport after they first met, he had boldly undressed her with his eyes. What embarrassed her then was how she had reacted to such an open once-over from a guy she didn't know. His looks were different now, but every so often, a hint of desire came through. Or was that just because she wanted to see what wasn't there? As much as she missed the touch of a man, the chances of Stephen Angelus arousing her other than in her mind were nil.

Still, she couldn't deny the attraction. One kiss did not an overture make. What had made that kiss so memorable was how right it had felt. Not one to believe in the one man one woman theory, she nonetheless couldn't shake the instant bonding she had experienced. The man was a hard-nosed clod and yet she wanted him. There had to be something in that. No one else had gotten through to her. Some far superior in looks and temperament to Stephen had tried. So what had she done? Gotten the hots for a washed-up spy. That's what.

On impulse she took a couple of bottles of Cabernet Sauvignon from the shelf. She couldn't find any arsenic. The idea of relaxing by a warming fire sipping wine while Rambo got soaked by the elements sounded terrific. Blessing Rosemary for providing an abundant bankroll, Josie chatted amicably with the girl ringing up her order. Escaping Stephen for several hours was just what the doctor ordered.

The house was quiet. Her lord and master must be having so much fun he couldn't bear to come back and give her a hard time. Either that, or he was making copious notes on how to dump her for refusing to try pretending she had the agility of a mountain goat. Before putting the groceries away, she got a fire started in the living room fireplace. The fire was going nicely by the time she returned, glass of wine in hand, to settle on cushions she threw on the floor. She had no sooner gotten comfortable than she heard the back door slam. So much for peace and quiet.

"What do you think you're doing?"

A cat coming in from the rain looked better than he did. She had never seen him blanch beneath the ruddy toned complexion brought on by outdoor exposure.

"I'm having a glass of wine. Would you like one?" She couldn't resist baiting him.

"Alcohol is not suggested during training. It clouds the judgment."

His pious approach was beginning to set her teeth on edge. She purposefully took a deep sip of her wine.

"Is that so? Then they shouldn't have provided wine glasses. Maybe if you had been kind enough to share the training manual with me, I would have known not to indulge. It's too late now, isn't it?"

As he started toward her, she noticed he was limping. Was it possible for paragons of virtue to injure themselves?

"Where have you been?" he asked sharply, wincing from what must have been a painful knee or ankle.

"I went grocery shopping," she answered. "Your challenge to participate in today's suicide mission was out of line. Didn't you hear me say I was turning back?"

"No, I didn't."

Putting her glass of wine down next to the fire, she got to her feet and went over to him. Whether it was his look of dejection or the magnetism she felt emanating from him she couldn't be sure. Tugging at his jacket, she wordlessly started getting it off of him.

"That's a failing of yours that needs correcting," she said, dropping his jacket on the floor. "You never listen to me. Good grief, you're soaked clear through. Let's get you out of these wet things and see where you've hurt yourself."

A quick pull on the Velcro tabs loosened his foul weather pants. Unprepared for how the tight fitting thermal underclothing hugged his muscular body, she couldn't help but let her eyes linger where they shouldn't as she searched for the source of his injury. Bending to remove his heavy socks, she found the culprit. His left ankle was bruised and swollen. Carefully probing the skin, she could tell there were no broken bones. His feet had turned white from the cold.

"It's nothing," he insisted. "I just stepped on it wrong."

"Get off it," she demanded, pulling on his hand to get him to sit down. "I'll try to get some circulation going in your feet."

"That'll wait," he said softly. "Come here."

The strength of his arms enclosed her as his mouth connected with hers. Every horrible thought she had ever had about him vanished. An inquisitive tongue sought entry, stirring a thirst she had to quench. Each taste of him was more satisfying than the one before had been, drawing her closer until she couldn't stand the barrier between them.

Reaching to pull off his damp thermal turtleneck, she received no resistance. Rather, Stephen hurried to help, relieving of her sweatshirt as well. His cool torso quickly warmed as he brought her against him once more. She wasn't sure if it was he or she who sighed when her breasts came in contact with his chest. All she knew for certain was she wanted all of him and hang the consequences.

"We shouldn't," he began.

"But we will," she finished.

Needing no more encouragement, his mouth began exploring her face, pausing at the corners of her lips and at the base of her temples. In the meantime, she was free to wander over the wide expanse of his back with her hands, marveling at the muscular physique responding to her. He was much more intoxicating than the forgotten wine.

When his mouth moved on to her neck, she welcomed his tiny nips by putting her head back to give him free reign. Wherever his lips rested, she hoped he would linger so the sensations would never stop. Just when she thought he was going to avoid her breasts forever, his hands surrounded them both, gently helping each swelling nipple to its fullest extension. Skillful fingertips created patterns of anticipation that spread through her in a rush unlike any she had ever experienced before. She felt as though she had been waiting for Stephen all of her life and she was finally where she belonged.

"Touch me," he breathed. "Please."

What had happened to his pants was immaterial. The minute she reached for him, she knew his need was equal to hers. The sleek, glossy surface grew harder yet as she investigated all of him. His tongue progressed easily across her yearning nipples, sending a shudder through her. Arching toward the source of infinite indulgence, she continued to bring him closer to the final connection nothing would stop her from having. When he sought and found her most sensitive source of pleasure, it was exactly as if he knew every secret of her desire.

Surely she would not be able to hold on much longer if she let him continue to kindle the flame he had built within her. Too weak to stop him, she let him take her higher and higher. Regardless of what his feelings about her were, he was loving her.

Exquisitely. Perfectly. Unforgettably.

"Open your eyes," he whispered.

She always kept them shut to preserve her fantasies. When she opened them and looked at Stephen, she knew he was her fantasy.

"I want to see you and you to see me," he told her.

His face said it all. Suffused with passion, nothing was hidden from her. His eyes, sometimes so hard and cold, were full of the tenderness he was showing to her. Positioning himself above her, he didn't stop massaging her sensitive nub so close to exploding. The dewy moisture she could feel coming from him signaled the urgency of his entry.

Sinking into her gradually, he had only filled her partially when the convulsions of her climax began. With repeated onslaughts, the surging crests washed over her. Letting the impact engulf him, Stephen waited before going the rest of the way. Then he went deeper and deeper into her. Filling her completely. Possessing her entirely.

Matching the rhythm of his final ride, Josie felt her own reaction beginning again. No man had ever been able to bring that out in her. Seeing her look of surprise, Stephen stepped up the pace, smiling down at her. She gave herself over to absorbing him, claiming each withdrawal and reentry tightly. Wrapping her legs around him as he made his final plunge, she held him to her as his heat began to flow.

Now it was her turn to watch him experience the effects of their mating. No words could describe what she was feeling and she was fairly certain the same went for him. She didn't need to be told what they had just shared was most assuredly not suggested during training or any other time. Make believe and reality had collided. Maybe Stephen could still separate the two. It was beyond her.

"Did you say something about wine?" he asked, carefully adjusting his weight without withdrawing from her.

"There's only one glass," she answered, still trying to believe what had just happened wasn't a dream.

"I've been known to share," he said, bringing her glass to his lips.

"I thought you said alcohol was not suggested during training," she reminded him.

"Some rules don't make any sense," he replied, burying his face in her hair. "You realize, of course, this sheds a whole new light on your budding career as an operative."

"Oh?" she teased. "I thought you were helping me to learn the finer points of copulation. That is what husbands and wives do, isn't it?"

"You don't need any instructions, Josie. Trust me. I've wanted to be like this with you since almost the first moment I saw you."

"I hope you don't mind me saying you took a most circuitous route dragging me all over the countryside. A simple I'm hot for your bod would probably have been easier on both of us. You really reached the nadir today."

"You're completely right."

"I am?" Maybe he had hurt more than his ankle.

"Completely. That was wrong of me. I'm sorry."

She was stunned. It seemed so out of character for him to apologize.

"Then are we finished with the physical part of my discipline?" she finally managed to ask.

"That depends," he replied, slowly drawing circles around her breasts with his finger, causing a reaction she couldn't control.

"On what?" she got out with difficulty.

Under no circumstances would she squirm. Regardless of what he was doing, she didn't trust him enough yet to expect him to play fair.

"On what your definition is of physical," he answered, dipping his head to taste the rigid peaks he had created.

"I was referring to your swell imitation of boot camp," she informed him. Her hand instinctively moved to the back of his head, spurring him on to continue what he was doing.

He stopped. She wanted more.

"But you were so obliging." His grin was infuriately wicked.

"You didn't give me a choice."

"It kept me from doing what we've just done, among other things."

"What's wrong with what we just did?"

"Oh, God, Josie." He rolled away from her. "We aren't supposed to be fucking, for Christ's sake."

Had it been anyone else, she would have sworn he was blushing. The kindest thing she could do was put on her clothes and go back to pretending. She wasn't feeling charitable.

"That's a real drag," she told him, extending both arms behind her head, knowing full well the movement accentuated her swollen breasts.

He had started to sit up. The one part of him he couldn't restrain betrayed how his body was reacting to hers.

"Personal involvement is to be kept to a minimum," he repeated, needlessly as far as she was concerned.

He was struggling to retain the cool, detached persona he had been previously. She wasn't ready to let that happen yet.

"If you can show me where in the manual it says thou shalt not fornicate with thine assigned partner, I'll try to delude myself into thinking I have an overactive imagination." She sat up so she could look into his eyes. "Otherwise," she could feel her voice start to tremble, "I think both of us are adult enough to handle ourselves appropriately when we are required to do so."

"Meaning?" He wasn't going to let her off easily, but he wasn't having any luck getting his mask back in place. With all pretense dropped, how much he wanted precisely what she wanted was written all over him.

"Our only concern needs to be that the assignment isn't compromised by whatever else we may do." She tried to control her voice with borderline results. "As long as we keep things in perspective, we'll be fine. Personally, I think we'll be much more convincing as Theo and Althea."

"You realize, of course, that's a completely flawed rationalization."

He reached for her, quickly covering her body with his. She held him as closely as he was holding her.

"Can you come up with something better?" she asked.

"I think I already have," he replied, nibbling his way across her throat, "except for one thing. This floor is hard. Will it be your bed or mine?"

Chapter Seven

❖

She fit into the curve of his body like she had always been there. Gossamer skin aligned with his, a source of warmth and pleasure he could not let go. Years of training jeopardized by a woman he was prepared to despise. God knows he'd put her through hell to rid himself of the temptation.

At first, she represented only a body. Someone he could use to appease the voracious sexual appetite built up over months of sporadic neglect. Anyone would have done, of course, but Josie had nothing in common with his past crop of choices. They were hardened professionals performing a service. They had suited him at the time. Josie brought out an itch no whore could scratch to his satisfaction. He had wanted to arouse the passion in her. By doing so, he could then sate his own.

Where did that leave him? In a pickle, that's where. A woman such as she expected hearts and flowers. He had none to give. There had been too many days of living day to day. Making plans wasn't part of the deal. If Josie couldn't accept that, he'd withdraw from the assignment. The look on Thaddeus' face when he told him would be worth the shame of owning up to an unwritten departmental indiscretion. Josie moved. His meandering mind clicked off.

"Are you awake?" he asked.

"No," she answered, sensually rubbing against him.

"How 'bout an invigorating hike," he suggested, biting the earlobe closest to him.

She turned in his arms, settling a seductive leg between his. The look of innocence that drove him wild started his arousal the minute she touched him.

"How 'bout exercising this dandy dingle dangle instead?" she countered, rubbing her thigh along the length of him.

Hot desire came instantly, made stronger by her fingers adding their special brand of enticement, leaving no part of him untouched. The tender flesh of her breasts flowed beneath his hands. Obedient centers sprang to life, beckoning his mouth so he could taste her. Gradually he was learning, gauging progress by the lows moans in her throat, while holding back to be sure she was ready for him.

Stroking each nipple in turn with his tongue, he reached for the thoroughly moistened center of her sex. As he fondled the elusive target, Josie increased the pressure on his shaft, bringing him to the edge of orgasm. She had already proved to him how she could suspend him at the precarious pinnacle, making the final moments rise to a screaming intensity. Then, she was astride him, placing herself on his ready tip.

Deliberately making his entry as slow as possible, she took him into her bit by bit, letting the friction mount until he didn't think he could take any more. He moved his hands to her waist to get her to go faster. The gesture was useless. Josie was controlling him and she knew it. With her gaze locked on his, she started to move her pelvis, riding him hard, consuming him. The more he tried to hold back, the more savagely she picked by the tempo. He couldn't wait. The coming began, involving all of him with such an incredible force he thought the flood would never stop. At the peak of his pleasure, she joined him, rocking back and forth as the impact struck. He pulled her down against his chest, filling his arms with her.

Once with a woman, always. Twice, perhaps. More than that was doubtful. So what was it about Josie Giltner that had unlocked an insatiable desire he satisfied only to have it come on again more strongly than the time before? Turning them over so her head rested on the pillow, he searched her face for some clue. All he saw was a beautiful woman whose lips he had bruised with his kisses looking back at him. Her violet eyes shown with passion, but gave him no answers. He ran his fingers over the delicate skin of her cheeks, chafed by the stubble of his beard.

"I should have been more careful," he said.

"Is that a Freudian slip?" she asked, smiling up at him.

Was it possible for a woman to be that collected? He'd never met one. Something was out of focus. Here he was, still reeling from the effects of finally having what he wanted, only to be thrown off balance by her all over again.

"You're taking your advice much too seriously," he chided, continuing to caress her face because he liked the way she reacted. "We're examining perspectives. Remember?"

"Will you send up a flare when that guy you sometimes are is getting ready to make an appearance?" she asked.

So that was it. No wonder. His treatment of her had been erratic at best, from one end of the scale to the other. He owed her an explanation. How could he do that without letting her into places he'd rather she not be? Oh, what the hell. She was already there anyway.

"That guy made such an ass of himself, he's slunk off to a dark corner where he belongs, Josie. I can't promise you I won't be hard-nosed about things, but I do promise not to work against you anymore." He twisted a curl of her hair around his finger, talking to it as much as to her. "I should be ashamed of myself for not being able to restrain myself. Oddly enough, I'm not. My only concern is what repercussions may crop of as a result of our having sex together."

He purposefully did not use the term making love although it may well have been apt. The least amount of confusion, the better. Still being buried in her aside, he had to appear detached. Exactly how Josie felt was hard to gauge.

"What's there to be concerned about?" she asked, actually looking surprised. "Are you afraid I'll misinterpret your motives? It that it?"

"To a degree, yes."

"Don't be, Stephen. I'm just as guilty as you are. You didn't force yourself on me. I wanted to do exactly what we've done, not because I'm confused about why it is we're here, but because I'm hopelessly attracted to this body of yours, great pecs and all." She poked at his chest as she spoke before linking her hands behind his neck. "I won't lie to you and say I wouldn't look forward to an eternity of having you around to turn me on. Since that's out of the question, I'll make do with whatever time together we have."

Perhaps she was deferring to his devotion to duty or she saw him only as a good lay. Why didn't either of those options sit well with him?

"It's good to have that settled," he said, still unconvinced. "Do you mind me saying you're a lot more woman than I know what to do with?"

"I don't mind you saying it," she told him, "as long as you realize I don't believe a word of it. Anyone who can start a fire as quickly as you do can hardly claim to be a shrinking violet. You've got the pleasuring part down pat."

It's everything else I can't handle, he thought. Why is it with you I get notions I can?

Aloud he said, "what you're neglecting to mention is the part you play in that," kissing the small lobes of her ears he exposed by pushing her hair behind them. "I haven't even begun to know you."

"You mean there's more?" She fluttered her lashes in mock amazement. "If that's the case, we'd better have some fortification. You stay right where you are. I'll be back in a jiffy."

Sliding out of his arms, she bounced off of the bed, displaying the full elegance of her slim nakedness. She didn't flaunt her beauty. She simply wore it without pretense. There was almost as much gratification in watching her as there was in arousing her. Almost. Not quite. The truth was, of course, Josie was a woman out of his league. No matter how hard he tried, he could never be the man she deserved. Both his job and his temperament wouldn't allow sharing. There was no room for her in his life. Why then, did he feel empty by the ordinary act of her leaving the room?

He could hear her rustling around downstairs in the kitchen. Existing on passion only stretched so far. Another variety of hunger couldn't be ignored. He had to concede without Josie's culinary expertise, their first week together would have been a total dud. Who's fault was that? His, damn it. She'd kept up her part of the bargain much better than he. Did she have what it took to see the whole deal through? Who could say? In the final analysis, the fact remained she was his partner and he'd spent entirely too much time adjusting to that. As to their literal interpretation of spousal relations, the old adage that each assignment added a broader dimension to one's experience had blundered into a new vista. How well he could handle the risks involved remained to be seen.

The sight of Josie coming through the door with a tray full of great smelling food had a tendency to distract his concentration considerably. How much her nakedness contributed to that, he was not prepared to tackle at the moment. Something more mundane was his best defense.

"I think Ted is probably better than Theo," he said, helping her put the tray down on the bed. "God, this looks good. What do you think?"

"It's up to you," she replied, modestly covering his greatest source of pleasure with a napkin. "Dig in."

"Thanks. I will." He greedily tried everything in sight. Manners be damned. "I hadn't realized I was so hungry."

"You keep giving me such wide openings for making wisecracks" she told him, wiping a drip off of his chin. "I'll let that one go by on general principle. Your ankle really should be wrapped."

He looked at the bruised offender he had done his best not to think about. Forget the chagrin of his klutzy performance. He was the pro. Pros didn't make dumbshit mistakes. They were above all that. Pros watched where they were going instead of picturing battered bodies lying crumbled in a ditch. Pros didn't get a hard on looking at naked partners with grape jelly on her cheek either. Or if they did, they sure as hell figured out a way to hide it.

"You're probably right," he agreed. "I guess I had other things on my mind. Is there any more coffee?"

"Don't avoid the issue," she insisted, reaching for the thermos container of coffee. "As soon as we're finished here, it's Ace bandage time for you."

"That may be awhile," he informed her, holding out his cup. "I have the strongest feeling we can find better things to do."

Downing the coffee in one gulp, he calming dipped his finger into the grape jelly and proceeded to decorate her breasts, paying special attention to the absorbing nipples. Before he could stop her, Josie whisked away the woefully inadequate camouflage under which his blossoming erection was unsuccessfully hiding.

"My, my. What have we here," she asked impishly. "Is this an object for body art?"

His lack of reply was no deterrent to her. Busy licking away at his own graffiti, that she would join in the game so zealously didn't occur to him. When she bent to remove her artwork, he got lost in the thundering hold of fierce sensations she was creating.

His experience did not include freely given affection, which made the contact all the more powerful. Having always avoided allowing his emotions to get involved, letting them loose sneaked up on him. It wasn't as if he consciously gave up control. In the space of one night, what used to be was no longer good enough. Josie had unleashed a hunger in him only she could satisfy. Right now he was her prisoner, succumbing to a sweet torture surpassing simple release and moving into unchartered territory.

Her fingers judged his progress as she brought him closer to the final climb, extending the magnitude of arousal to an incomparable pitch. Losing his hands in the tangles of her hair, he made sure the encompassing warmth of her wouldn't leave him. Higher and higher she took him. Teasing. Tempting. Drawing out every stroke with exquisite care. The shout of triumph was his as the rush became a torrent erupting from him, leaving him limp from the impact. Assuring he was totally spent, Josie didn't leave him. He withdrew on his own.

"Is the jelly all gone?" he asked, idly running his fingers over the lips that had just shown him matchless enjoyment.

"I think it's all used up," she replied.

"Pity. You wore it so well," he told her, bringing her face up to his. "You do the most unexpected things."

"Do I now?"

She looked at him as if she might be able to read the alien thoughts that suddenly came out of nowhere. Thoughts about having her all to himself. Thoughts about how he would feel if another man dared to touch her. Thoughts that she was his. Kissing her seemed like a good idea. She closed her eyes when they kissed, no longer looking into his soul.

The distinctive buzz of the FAX machine, which Thaddeus preferred to use for discreet communication rather than the Internet, startled them both. Whirring furiously, the interloper began to spit out page after page into the receiving tray. So much for romantic interludes. Duty called.

"Hold onto your hat," he told Josie. "It looks as though Thaddeus has sprung to life."

"He has a lot to say, doesn't he?" She started to gather up breakfast debris putting everything on the tray. "While he's communicating, I'll get rid of this stuff. And then, Ted," she emphasized the name, "I'm wrapping that ankle of yours."

"Nobody likes a wife who nags," he said, throwing his napkin at her. "Let's see how it feels after a shower."

"Suit yourself, mister big guy, but don't blame me if it gives you fits later on."

With a wiggle of her cute little ass, she bowed out of the room. Moving over to examine what had been sent to them, Stephen couldn't help but smile. Anyone would think Thaddeus knew Josie had passed the endurance part of her training and was ready for the next component of the process.

Now came the tedium. In a couple of days, both he and Josie might well prefer the outside, rain or no rain. In whatever time was allotted to them by Thaddeus, every minute detail pertaining to the couple they were bound to portray had to be committed to memory. There was no room for error. Mistakes could be fatal.

By the volume of the transmission, the Hartmanns had tweaked the imagination of the background staff. No simple, down-home folks would do for that bunch of fabricators. Depth was their specialty down to and including such trivial details as childhood diseases. Better to leave no stone unturned was their motto. He couldn't fault them. What he often thought was irrelevant fluff had saved his hide more than once.

The whole idea was that he and Josie would immerse themselves as completely as possible into the characters they were to play. The less they switched back and forth, the easier it was to keep up the ruse. As a solo act, he had mastered the art. With someone else in tow, it would be more difficult.

Drawback number one was Josie didn't consider herself much of an actress. That had to change. By hook or by crook, she had to get with the program. Could he regain his detachment? He had better start trying. Leaving the bed of love behind, he headed for the shower.

The FAX was quiet by the time he was through in the bathroom. He could not say the same for his ankle. The damn thing throbbed up a storm besides being sore as a boil. Funny how he had hardly noticed it until now.

"I see the shower's healing powers weren't up to the task."

She was sitting on the bed, which made been made, Ace bandage in hand, exhibiting no outward signs of their recent debauchery. Evidently, his prepared remarks, composed while he bathed as to how they would be expected to conduct themselves, weren't necessary.

"Staying off of it should do the trick," he said in a noble effort to downplay his clumsiness.

"That's a given," she answered, patting the space beside her. "Sit down and put your foot in my lap. Once I'm through, keeping it elevated would probably help considerably. You'll have a lot of time to sit. We've got a bunch of studying to do."

He sat. Arguing was pointless.

"Have you already started?" he asked, indicating the sheaf of papers beside her on the bed.

"I was reading something Thaddeus addressed to me about the more salient refinements of becoming someone else."

Wrapping his ankle as she talked, her face was hidden from him. He couldn't tell from her voice how she had absorbed what Thaddeus had said to her. What came through loud and clear was somewhere along the line, Josie had received first aid training, including how to bandage sprains.

"How do you feel about that part?" he asked.

Her face told the story. Thaddeus hadn't pulled any punches.

"I'm scared silly," she confessed.

She looked it. At least she was being honest. Many weren't.

"There's no harm in that," he assured her, forcing himself not to put his arm around her. "Better to be uncertain than overconfident."

"I'll take your word for it," she said. "It's not learning the part that scares me. It's pulling off the rest of it."

"Don't dwell on that now," he told her. "Work on the other first.

"Before we begin, I think you should know I had a dry run. I met our neighbor in the market yesterday. He knows our name. He called me Mrs. Hartmann."

His senses immediately sharpened. Was it all over before it began? Had she blown it?

"Oh?"

Keep cool. Let her talk.

"I played along as best I could, pretending I was who he thought I was. All he wanted to do was let us know this rain could trigger an emergency situation."

"How did he know who you were?"

Suspicion was second nature. Better to be safe than sorry.

"He has local connections. A sister-in-law has access to records. Mainly, I think he's just a harmless busybody trying to be helpful."

"Don't ever assume," Stephen cautioned her. "It's not recommended."

"Really, Stephen." She didn't hide her indignation. "Do you always look for enemies behind every tree?"

"That's why I'm alive."

How dare she question him? No one did that.

"In the heat of battle, I'm sure that's true. We aren't there yet. This is supposed to be a training situation." She paused as a thought struck her. "Isn't it?"

She was right. As much as he hated admitting it.

"Yes, Josie. It is. My point is how careful you need to be. Tell me exactly what he said or an equal facsimile of it."

She did. Her recall faculties could not be faulted nor could he quarrel with how she had responded to the old coot. All she needed to understand was further contact must be minimal. Any outside influence could cause the whole delicate structure of planning to fall apart.

"It sounds innocent enough," he conceded, deciding against a compliment for her performance. "No harm done. For obvious reasons, we never become involved in local affairs."

"Do you have any idea how sanctimonious you sound?" she asked. "Maybe you shy away from people for your own reasons, but don't include me in that."

What had he done wrong? All he was trying to do was protect her from a constant need to pretend she was someone else. She had no idea how much concentration that took. He shouldn't touch her. He had to, holding her shoulders in his hands as he turned her toward him. Staying detached was going to be a lot harder that he had thought.

"Some things you're going to have to trust me on, Josie."

The way she looked at him let him know trust was the one thing she didn't give easily. That he understood perfectly. Neither did he.

"I'm trying to, Stephen. Honest I am."

"It's tough for you," he empathized. "Trusting, I mean"

"If you had my track record, it would be hard for you too. I have to learn how to swing back and forth. You already know how."

"I've had a lifetime of experience," he admitted frankly. "Pretending isn't something I learned on the job. I just got better at it, that's all."

"You can't tell me anything personal, can you, Stephen?"

Nothing about what she was going to do bore any resemblance to being normal. How could he explain that?

"It isn't that I can't, Josie. After how we spent the night, I know this is going to sound ludicrous, but the less we know about each other, the safer it is."

"For whom?"

She had a point. What they were involved in was far from the complicated spy network into which he came and went as a code name with no identity. On the other hand, whether he liked it or not, when their time together was finished, he would walk away without looking back. That was how it was. No involvement. No commitment. End of conversation.

"There you have me," he allowed reluctantly. "It's habit, don't you see? Up until now, I've never known squat about the people with whom I've worked."

"How many of them did you kiss?"

"None. They weren't my type." Had she read too much into their physical attraction? Lord, he hoped not. "Maybe we've made a fatal mistake. It's my fault. I should never have touched you."

"You're touching me now," she reminded him. "I thought we already had the intimacy factor fully discussed. I'm not trying to rope you in, Stephen. All I want to know is a little more about the person I'm depending on to get me the rest of the way on this caper. Whether you want to admit it or not, you have a picture of me that falls somewhere short of the truth."

His hands clutched her shoulders more tightly. "I broke a rule on that," he told her. "I asked Thaddeus about you."

"That's unfair. I didn't ask him about you."

"You'll have to agree our situations were entirely different. At least you knew I had on the job training. All I wanted was some basic information. I wasn't interested in your pedigree."

"That's good. I don't have one, but I think you do."

"Do you know anything about horse breeding?" he asked.

"Not a thing," she answered. "Why?"

"Just curious."

"I doubt that. You had a specific reason for asking and I want to know why."

Josie could be quite insistent he was discovering. He'd opened the door. What harm was there in letting her in? He dropped his hands from her shoulders, putting them in his lap.

"Let me give you my totally biased opinion about the folks involved in equestrian pursuits. As a whole, they are opinionated, prejudiced, catty people who haven't risen much above the slave labor mentality of their ancestors. They deal in flesh. They make a lot of money. On the merit of their fortunes, they believe themselves to rank somewhere between God and the angels. A few of them seriously question the Lord's ability to run things."

"You don't like them," she translated, "but you were born into their midst."

"And raised accordingly," he added,

"I'll bet you were a hellion."

She was right. He had been.

"On the contrary," he protested, "I was a model child."

"Who resented authority, did your best to infuriate your elders, and knew the sting of a strap across your rear end."

"It was a belt," he corrected her, "with a heavy metal buckle."

Shock filled her eyes. Such punishment clearly was beyond her comprehension.

"Who?" she asked weakly.

"My father," he explained. "Whip a horse, whip a kid. It was all the same to him. You have to realize, Josie, that his rigid code of ethics was genetic. All thoroughbreds, human or otherwise, were better for being broken. It worked with my older brother. Why shouldn't it work with me?"

"Where is your brother now?"

"At the old homestead last I heard, drinking himself slowly to death and still trying to please the old man. My visits back there are rare, Josie, as is contact with my family."

"Where is there?"

"Not all that far from the Armatures, actually. About seventy-five miles due west."

"It was they who threw you off about me, wasn't it?"

"Guilty as charged," he agreed, holding up his hands in surrender.

"Then I rest my case," she declared, getting to her feet. "Misconceptions are insidious, Stephen. Let's not have any more of them, okay?"

Which misconceptions fell under her catch-all, he wasn't sure. She was trying as hard as he was to readjust herself back to a more neutral state with appropriate space between them. She might expect more than he had to give, but accusing her of being a clinging vine was definitely not in the picture.

"Exactly what are you suggesting?" he asked.

"Just be straight with me, Stephen, that's all. I'm scared. I admit it. Work with me instead of constantly trying to prove how much better you are. I'm not giving up, so you're wasting your time. I survived last week and I'll survive this, with or without your support. I'm going to my room now to start becoming Althea."

Either she wasn't expecting an answer from him or didn't care if he had one. Picking up her hefty pile of background material, she started for the door.

"Josie," he called after her.

She turned back. "yes?"

"What time is dinner?"

Her smile couldn't have been wider. "Earlier than usual, I think," she said. "Shall we say six?"

He stared at the empty doorway for some time after she was no longer there. She could bewitch him, stand up to him, and raise his hackles more quickly than anyone he had ever known. Her effect on him was nothing short of bewildering, a rather unsettling phenomenon if there ever was one. All he needed to do was concentrate on the job at hand. Why then, did her face, her lips, the translucence of her skin, her full, ripe breasts, and the surge he felt each time he entered her keep distracting him throughout the rest of the day?

Sitting across from her while they had dinner put him back in sync again. She looked over the rim of her wine class, daring him to repeat his warning about the advisability of mixing liquor into the training regimen. Her cooking was great as usual. He had no idea what he ate. Excusing herself when they were through, she left him to clean up as he had become accustomed to doing. He was acutely aware of her moving around in the room above him. Spending another night together was not going to happen. Her door was closed. His would be too.

After an hour of tossing and turning, his resolve weakened considerably. Was it possible she was in a similar predicament? Going to see wouldn't hurt. Had he been paying attention, he would have seen the light under her door. All he saw were those luminous eyes looking into his.

"You're late," she said, folding back the covers for him.

He turned out the light and climbed in beside her.

Chapter Eight

Althea Hartmann was a prig. No question about it. How she was supposed to have snared a husband who worshipped the ground she walked on defied logic to its breaking point.

"She's a blob," Josie complained to Stephen. "Nobody could be that pious and not be expected to walk on water."

"Are you sure she hasn't perfected that feat yet?" he teased, clearly enjoying Josie's character interpretation. "Remember, we want Porter Holloway to be sucked in by this broad."

"He'll probably ignore her like a dirty shirt. Are you sure I don't get a halo as a prop?"

"I'll check with wardrobe," he chuckled, leaning back in his chair.

He was being smug again. She hated it when he was smug.

"You're being unfair," she accused, feeling her control slowly slipping away as it was prone to do lately. "Playing goody-two-shoes just isn't my style. You get to be the strong, silent type, a set-up if I ever saw one. Why didn't they give me the easy part? Did you put them up to this?"

"I swear I didn't," he insisted. "You keep saying that. How often do I have to tell you that Porter goes for the woman, not the man?"

"Well, he'll sure be wasting his time with Althea. She's about as sexy as Mary Poppins. I know his background check says he has a roving eye, but unless we lighten her up, he's going to find her boring, banal, and uninspiring."

"Did it ever occur to you her piety is exactly the kind of hook we want? The man's an egomaniac. He thinks no woman can resist him. Althea will drive him up a wall."

"She's already driving me up a wall."

"Go outside and walk around for a bit," he suggested. "You always do better when you get away from this for a little while. Go on." He waved his hand toward the door. "Clear out the frustration. It's almost a nice day."

It was either that or scream. Grabbing her jacket, she escaped into the weak sunshine, taking deep breaths of the pine scented air to calm herself down. This business of assuming someone else's identity was much harder than she had expected it to be. Not that she had thought becoming Althea would be easy. What was the use? She hadn't thought. Period.

Damn you, Jason, for putting me in this position regardless of whether you meant to or not. And damn you, Stephen Angelus, for showing me love when I needed it so badly. You're trying your best to steer clear of having any misunderstandings about what the outcome will be with us. I don't know what to make of it any more than you do, but I think we've found something neither of us is going to want to let go. As disinterested as you pretend to be, you give yourself away when you come to my bed and can't get through every night without us being one. It isn't just sex to you, Stephen. It's more than that and you know it.

How am I supposed to cope with that and Althea too? Wait. I've got it. Why didn't I think of this before? Little Miss Priss has a deep, dark secret those guys in Washington were too embarrassed to spell out in detail. She's the picture of purity with her clothes on. Take them off and she's the last of the red hot mamas. Behind that tight little smile is a bedroom vamp who keeps old Ted so hard it hurts. Yes. That's it. She finally has a redeeming feature.

Now then, what about Stephen? He isn't my type. I can't imagine what attracted me to him. I should have seen through his veneer. No matter what he says, that genealogy of his comes out of his pores. He carries himself like gentry. He's arrogant like gentry. As much as he's tried to shed the image, he can't. And yet, there's another side to him that's tender, giving, and kind. Yes. Kind. He'd hate to hear me say that, but he is. No one has needed kindness more than I have these past weeks. Whenever I sag, he's there to bolster me up. I would never have gotten this far without him.

Where does that leave me? Confused. What's wrong with me anyway? Jason promised me the moon and I thought it was love. Stephen hasn't promised me anything and I don't want to think about living without him. Fat chance. The man sees the world through the eyes of his job. Such a convenient dodge to hide behind. And what am I doing thinking he should be any other way? Am I any better?

This job is all I've got. Jason's legacy isn't going to pay itself off. So, enough romantic notions. Back to Althea, the paradigm of all that's holy. Long may she reign.

"Feeling better?" he asked as she walked into the kitchen.

"Why, Ted, how you do go on. I've never felt better in my life. There's nothing like hours of enlightening meditation to shore up the soul and lift the spirits."

"Hours? I could swear you weren't gone more than fifteen or twenty minutes."

"That's in addition to spending most of last night on my knees."

"Your knees, my love, were indeed pointed toward heaven, but I'm here to tell you there wasn't a line of communication open to the Almighty as far as I could tell."

"Why, Ted, you rascal, you. I do declare you bring out the devil in me."

"My pleasure," he said bowing deeply. "Is this your way of telling me you're ready to go out into the big, wide world and practice with real people?"

Now, that was an aspect she hadn't considered as yet. "Go out?" she echoed, a shiver of panic running up her spine. "I don't see how I could. I don't have a thing to wear."

"You must have been a real crowd pleaser as the grocery store," he said.

"Huh?"

"No wonder Mr. Whoseits took such a shine to you, Mrs. Hartmann. I'm surprised he hasn't been camped out on our doorstep."

"Now you stop your teasing right there, Mr. Hartmann. I mean I don't have anything to get spiffied up. Somebody told me I wouldn't be needing any of that."

"Well, shame on that someone. I guess we'll have to go shopping then."

"Mercy me," she hedged. "I wouldn't know where to start."

"That's why you married me," he said with a leer. "With my talent for research, I've scouted out a fine selection of locations from which to choose."

Of course he would. Raking her brain for some excuse, feeble or otherwise, to avoid the inevitable, Josie came up empty handed. Althea loved to shop. In fact, according to her bio, committed to memory by now, the woman had an unbridled passion for spending money. The choice was either break out of character and beg off or bite the bullet and get on with what she was being paid to do.

"Well, why didn't you say so?" she said brightly. "I can be ready in two shakes of a lamb's tail."

Whether Stephen approved of her brief flash of courage wasn't as important to her as being able to pull off the first test. Being himself or Ted, her tightlipped partner was miserly with praise of any kind. His quick reflexes to point out her mistakes had to be patterned after his father. Underneath the contempt expressed toward the elder statement of the clan, there was at the same time a strong resemblance between them except for one thing. Stephen was never cruel. A severe taskmaster, yes. But never cruel.

The dress shops he took her to were all located in small communities the names of which meant nothing to her. What both the merchandise and the locations had in common could be described in one word. Money. Althea didn't look at price tags. Josie did while keeping up her assumed personality. Pretending to like what she was doing quickly became a stretch. Rosemary would have been proud. An hour at best had been Josie's previous limit of endurance. Althea plunged ahead for almost five hours, taking conspicuous consumption to unheard of heights.

Ted suggested calling it a day, pointing out a restaurant where they could have dinner. How Stephen had fared throughout the shopping spree was anyone's guess. The bland demeanor he wore so casually revealed nothing. Pert smile in place, Althea gave in to her husband with a Pollyanna artificiality that made Josie want to gag. A stiff shot of any variety of hard liquor would have helped considerably. Althea, of course, exemplary clod that she was, never touched the stuff. The quality of the food, along with having the shopping glut behind her, almost made up for the drink she wanted. Almost. Not quite.

"Excellent dinner, don't you think so, darling?"

He rested his hand on hers, making a fine show of the devoted husband. How much was real and how much wasn't?

"Delicious," she agreed as the well-trained waiter appeared to take their plates away.

"Will there be anything else?" the waiter asked.

"Two coffees," Stephen replied. "No cream. No sugar."

Josie used both. Althea didn't.

"May I bring you a dessert menu?"

Before Stephen could open his mouth, Josie said yes. He had ordered dinner for her without consultation. If she couldn't drink, at least she could have something sinfully chocolate to make up for the void. For the first time since her afternoon as Althea began, there was no need to fake how she felt.

"Are you sure you don't want any?" she asked, extending the dish toward Stephen.

"Maybe a bite," he conceded.

Scooping up a generous offering, she leaned across the table to feed it to him. As he opened his mouth, their eyes met. The man of a few words didn't hide behind an oblique front as he was prone to do. His frank look of admiration had nothing to do with Ted Hartmann. The urge to blow off Althea got stronger the more she basked in the first real sign that Stephen cared.

No. She didn't dare. Like her dessert, she would savor the moment. Up to this point, falling out of character had always been her move. Now it was up to him. She'd carry the ruse through the ride back and into bed if necessary. It would serve Stephen right. Let him have a go at wondering if the woman he pampered with infinite skill was as taken with his attention as she appeared to be. The welcome sight of the house came into view.

Keeping up the silly chatter that was supposedly part of Althea's personality, Josie grabbed as many shopping bags as she could from the back seat of the car. The evidence of obscene overindulgence also filled the trunk.

"It will take me hours to get everything organized," she chirped, doing her best imitation of looking forward to the dreaded process.

"Time out," Stephen begged, making the sign of a T with his hands. "Fluttering Southern women never did appeal to me and I'm more than willing to honor the fact that you have their most annoying qualities down pat."

"Why, thank you, kind sir," Josie stammered, hardly able to believe the combination of a compliment from him along with his withdraw from the ever courtly Ted. "Can we take all of these things back?"

"I'll ignore you asked," he replied, opening the trunk. "Althea without an appropriate wardrobe would be like Miss America without her crown."

"Are you sure you didn't insist on giving her a look that's just a shade too provocative?"

"Let's get all of these things into the house," he said, ignoring her question. "I have something to show you."

The shopping bags covered her bed in no time at all. Following Stephen back down the stairs, she marveled at his ability to pop in and out of Ted so easily. She had all she could do to stop the sugar coated accent of the pampered woman who promoted a life of benevolence to others while espousing exactly the opposite. The best part of pretending to be Althea, she had found, was getting away from more than a few harsh realities not even Stephen could completely obliterate.

Going into the living room, he went to the CD player. On top of the machine was a package she hasn't noticed there before. He took a disc out of the wrapping and placed it in the machine.

"Dirty movies?" she asked.

"You could say that," he answered. "Great quality it isn't, but it's hard to get the correct light and shading when the subject doesn't know he's being filmed. Welcome to the side of Porter Holloway the good people he leads never see."

The focus could have been sharper and the grainy black and white picture had a tendency to jiggle. What came through distinctly was the epitome of a person who had no scruples much less an interest in any aspect of Christian charity. Although it was difficult to hear every word, what could be deciphered might easily have been dialogue from an expletive laden Hollywood script. The few times she had seen clips of Porter, his tones were rounded and his message had always concerned the brotherhood of man according to an interpretation she found confining. That aside, the man had seemed sincere in spite of the fact Rosemary often said his ilk chose their flocks selectively.

Away from the bright lights and public view, Porter looked more like a weasel than a righteous apostle of the faith. His vocabulary was limited to four-letter words aimed at numerous enemies, seen and unseen. The scope of the inner circle had shrunk to a very select few with Porter himself as the main recipient of earthly rewards. From the sound of the recorded conversation, Porter was closing in on possessing an arsenal a number of corrupt regimes would gladly pay top dollar to call their own.

"Who took that film?" she asked as soon as the picture faded into a snowy demise.

"One of the best in the business," Stephen said. "I've worked with him several times. It's taken him months to get into the inner sanctum. Porter is not a very trusting sort."

"How did he get where he is?" Josie asked. "That's what I want to know."

"Ignorance and desperation are the main ingredients. One of the most popular bandwagons for the dregs of society is to claim they have seen the light. We don't know all that much about Porter's background. He more or less crawled out of the woodwork several years ago. His fabricated past has held up well because he did a thorough job of eliminating pesky loose threads who might have ratted on him. We now know he was a bit player in a fringe black market group that operated mainly in Eastern Europe."

"Supplied by whom?"

"Various sources, but military establishments work the best. Our armed forces are notorious for waste that costs millions. That's where Porter learned his trade."

"Where?"

"In the army. Pilfer a little here, pilfer a little there. We don't pay our soldiers very well, you know. A guy has to supplement his income. Getting caught doesn't matter. After a dishonorable discharge, the pickings were better than ever. He knew the system, so he just set himself up as a private entrepreneur supplying bigger fish. He got good at it. An aptitude for languages helped. I'm not sure how many countries wanted him. Probably all of the ones whose passports he so cleverly forged. Careful alterations of his appearance took place over time. When he was ready to step up to the biggest gamble of his career, he had become a new man."

"Who is he?"

"His real name is Bobby Leland. According to military records, he was a high school drop out with a short history of petty theft. No family to speak of, raised by his grandmother. She died years ago. After he was booted out of the army, details are a little sketchy."

"Was there ever a real Porter Holloway?" Josie asked, still digesting everything Stephen had said.

"Yes, indeed. An outstanding cover if ever there was one. The Holloway family crowded into the Mayflower along with every other upstanding ancestor to touch American soil. I've always been amazed how such a small ship accommodated so many passengers. Porter's forefathers were shopkeepers who made a name for themselves as able merchandising folks. Down through the generations, a reasonable fortune was amassed. Gradually, the family petered out, to a reclusive final member who kept to himself behind the walls of a mansion of sorts, rarely showing his face.

"All kinds of devious possibilities come to mind with that," Josie said.

"And Bobby tried them all. The one he settled on had vestiges of some truth. The last of the line, Nicholas Holloway by name, left a rather strange will. In it, he made a reference to his issue, none of which he had as far as anyone knew. Speculation settled on a woman Nicholas was known to have paid court to in his younger years. The general opinion was she had rejected his attention. But what if she hadn't?"

"I think I see where this is leading," she said.

"I'm sure you do. From the bowels of nowhere Porter was born. Carlotta Mannerly, the object of the old man's attention, had moved away from the area and fallen on hard times. Buried in a pauper's grave, she left no history or messy details to spoil Bobby's story. What Porter spouts as his humble beginnings is firmly supported by a forged birth certificate and fabrications cleverly submerged in just enough believability to make them plausible."

"Did he lay claim to the estate?"

"Pure Porter? Perish the thought. All he wanted was his so called birth right. Let the named charities have what they so richly deserved. Worldly goods, he claimed, were of no interest to him."

"I'll bet."

"He had bigger fish to fry. What Nicolas had left in the way of a fortune, while substantial, wasn't nearly enough for Porter's purposes. All he wanted was a platform and he finally found one ready made in the Christian right movement organization needing only a few minor adjustments."

"Such as?"

"The old guy who was running the show of the group Porter chose, unbeknownst to him, needed a successor. Enter Porter to salivate in the right places, quickly endearing himself to a naïve elderly gentleman whose faith, though narrow, was heartfelt."

"So Porter got rid of him?" she guessed.

"Bingo. Proving he killed the poor fellow would be far from easy. Natural causes or not, I'm inclined to believe nature was amply pushed ahead of the appointed time. Those who dared to suggest someone other than Porter should take over the helm fell out of favor before they could kick up too much of a fuss. With a clever combination of chutzpah and silver tongued oratory, Porter grabbed support from the largest segment of the admission paying crowd."

The pieces were falling into place. Where they were headed set Josie's teeth on edge.

"The women," she groaned. "He went after the women."

"Mainly certain women," Stephen corrected, "especially those with too much money and not enough good sense whose do-gooder mentalities flitted from pillar to post. Porter made sure his girls didn't stray. Emotional blackmail is one of his specialties."

"Swell. And you're sending me into that?"

"Not I," he assured her. "If you recall, I advised against it."

"That's right. You did," she agreed, hating herself for giving him the opening. "Don't take what I said as a sign of waffling. I'm not. All I'm doing is acknowledging I recognize how dangerous this whole business is."

Darn. Her recovery wasn't bad, but was it good enough to convince Stephen?

"The difference between you and them," he said, showing no outward reaction to the slapdash justification for her momentary lapse, "is insight. You know what you're up against. They blindly blundered in, ignorant of the consequences."

While she got to blunder in with her eyes wide open. Suddenly she felt much less prepared than Porter's innocent victims. She would reason her way out. That should do it.

"Why does he need Althea?" she asked. "Doesn't he have a big enough harem?"

"In essence, yes. What Althea represents, along with Ted, is a quicker means to an end. Both his and ours. Nothing talks louder than oodles of cash on hand. By the time he figures out he's been had, he'll be in the pokey and you'll be safely out of his reach."

"What happens to all of those clothes?" she asked, trying to bring some perspective to the totally surreal predicament she had gotten herself into.

"Josie," Stephen said softly, putting his arms around her, "there isn't anything rational about this. All props are returned when we're through. Don't try to put an ordinary spin on it. That isn't how the game is played."

Safe in his arms, she believed him. Convincing herself she could feel the same on her own two feet was a bit of a stretch.

"How have you stood it all these years, Stephen?"

"It beat the alternative by a mile."

She settled back a bit so she could look up at him. To her surprise, he was being quite sincere. Did he honestly believe undercover work had more going for it than a hundred other routes he might have taken?

"You can't tell me that joining the family enterprise was your only other choice."

"At the time I thought it was, Josie. I found another niche. It suited me."

"It suits you having nothing that's yours?"

As soon as the words were out, she regretted them. How Stephen lived his life was none of her business. Now he'd crawl into his shell for sure. Except he didn't. He continued to hold her.

"Better nothing than something you don't want, Josie. I had to get away as far as I could, beyond the extensive influence my father had. There may have been a senator or two in his pocket, but he hadn't considered our nation's security to be in need of his meddling. Do I regret what I did? Sometimes I do. Like right now when I wonder if I could ever make it in what is termed a normal life."

"What makes you think you couldn't?"

"Mainly, I never did very well at it in the first place. In case you haven't noticed, I'm not the easiest guy to get along with."

"You have your moments," she answered, snuggling closer to him. "Is it written somewhere that in order to have a normal life you have to get along with everyone?"

He rested his head on hers and once again, she thought he might choose to close her out. When he finally spoke, his voice was ragged from the effort.

"I used to be better at it, Josie. There was even a time when I thought I could run the Angelus stables and raise superior stock. Contrary to what you may think, a large chunk of that operation belongs to me. Having nothing isn't my problem. Having too much is."

He didn't elaborate and she couldn't think of a way she might encourage him to tell her more. The fact he had told her anything at all was a huge departure from his usual practice. Enclosed in his arms the way she was, extemporaneous background details could wait for another time. As their lips met, she was dimly aware it had started to rain again.

And it kept on raining. Continuously. How the ground could hold so much water boggled the mind. Tempers started to flare up, hemmed in by the aura of depression the weather enforced. They were as prepared as they ever were going to be. Both of them were suffering from cabin fever. Each succeeding deluge began to trigger warning signs of what was in store if a much-needed break in the weather didn't come soon. Over Stephan's objectives, Josie closely followed the local news.

"What's going on around us in immaterial," he told her. "Our priority is to be ready at a moment's notice to get on with what we were sent here to do."

"You can't be serious." She couldn't believe he could be so callous. "Our job isn't going to mean squat if we're buried under a ton of mud."

"That isn't our concern," he insisted. "Thaddeus employs specialists to keep an eye on local conditions for us. We're not in any danger. If we were, we'd be out of here."

"Maybe we're fine," she countered, unable to accept such a cavalier attitude, "but what about the people who aren't?"

"They aren't our problem. All of our energy has to be centered on the assignment. There is no room for anything else. Besides, Althea doesn't give a damn about the plight of those less fortunate than she is. You're not staying in character."

Althea was fast becoming a royal pain in the butt. In his current pompous ass guise, Stephen wasn't exactly scoring points either.

"Would you believe she's had a change of heart?" she asked.

Deep inside, Josie knew Stephen was right. She could do Althea to the hilt and had. What she couldn't do was close out the world around her like he could.

"Don't be ridiculous," he mocked at her.

That did it. He'd gone too far. The strain of the training held them in its grip. She wasn't about to back down anymore.

"What I'm being," she told him flatly, "is nothing more than humanly responsive to a situation we're in the middle of whether you admit it or not. You go right ahead playing super spy of the year. That's your bag. As hard as I try, I'll never be able to sit idly by, ignoring real events while I pretend to be someone else."

"Might I suggest you start learning that before you blow everything we've spent weeks perfecting?"

His voice had taken on a decidedly testy edge. Instead of deferring to him, she dug in her heels.

"You may suggest anything you please. Just don't ever presume you can control my mind. Althea Hartmann lives and breathes because of me. You've tried every trick in your dirty little book to trip me up and none of them have worked. If you think for one minute I can't carry her off regardless of the circumstances, then you haven't gotten to know me very well."

"Just what is it you have in mind?" he asked, barely disguising his anger.

"Nothing specific," she taunted him, gaining strength by successfully standing up to the stranger he could so quickly become. "If I think of something, I'll let you know."

"Don't go getting any ideas about joining the bucket brigade to hold back the flood," he warned.

"Until we're instructed to leave here, I'll rely on my own resourcefulness, not yours." His eyes narrowed as she went on. "You're good in the field, but you wouldn't know compassion if it walked up and bit you."

"I don't have time for compassion."

"More's the pity. Someday you may wish you had."

Turning quickly, she stomped out of the room, escaping up the stairs. Not once, in all of the weeks they had been in the mountains, had she locked her door. He could easily break it down. She knew that. All she wanted was a device to close him out. Nowhere in her instructions did it say he was always to have the last word. If she didn't sort out her thoughts about him before too long, frustration was going to get the better of her.

How was it possible to be in total harmony as lovers and at each other's throats more often than not the rest of the time? Especially lately. They had gotten over the first hump when he grudgingly began to respect her. At each successive step, he had seemed more accepting. Therein lay the problem. He couldn't or wouldn't tell her so. She had kept trying to convince herself their nights made up for everything. Now that was no longer true. She wanted more. She wanted him to love her.

There. The truth was out at last for whatever good it did her. The sooner she faced facts, the better. Too much of her life had been taken up chasing dreams that had no chance of coming true. If she doubted how harsh reality could be, all she had to do was think of Jason.

He was behind her, just as Stephen would be as soon as she could manage it. She didn't blame him. Not really. He was doing his job the same way he always did with what she took to be one major difference. Her.

How come he could handle it and she couldn't? So he had years of training under his belt. So what? No one could expect her to control herself in kind. Could they? The time had long since gone by when she was forced to face the fact she'd gotten in a lot deeper than she should have. Not only with Stephen. The job was all wrong too. No matter how good the money was, the price wasn't worth the aggravation. A deal was a deal. Althea would perform as required if called upon to do so. When that was done, she'd resign and find something else.

Having put her emotional affairs in order, Josie felt much better. Unlocking her door, she waited for Stephen to come to her, fully believing he would. She was wrong. He didn't come that night or the following one either. On the third day, Joseph Cooper came to the house.

"If you walk out of here, you can kiss the project good-bye," Stephen warned.

"Go to hell," she shot back at him before slamming the door behind her.

Chapter Nine

❦

With only the sound of the rain pounding down, the place was unnaturally quiet. Righteously lugging his large bundle of outmoded beliefs with him, Stephen roamed the rooms over and over, always returning to hers. She kept her place the same way she kept herself. Precisely. All of Althea's trappings were arranged carefully, totally separated from the clothes Josie had brought with her. As far as he knew, no one had told her to maintain a strict line of demarcation to keep herself in perspective. She just knew with that incredible instinct that never failed to knock his socks off.

He should have complimented her, he supposed. Why didn't he? He knew the answer all too well. The conditioning not to offer praise was buried so deeply within him, he couldn't shake the words he'd heard repeated so often.

"Only cowards need encouragement, boy. Or poor, dumb animals. You give horses rewards to encourage behavior. It's different with people. They learn best when you keep pushing them harder and harder. Don't expect any coddling from me, Stephen. Go to your mother for that."

"It's his kind of love, sweetheart," she told him, brushing the drooping hair off of his forehead. "You must not think otherwise." In itself, her voice could soothe him. "You will be a more gentle master than he is, I know. He holds on to a code no longer in vogue. There is much you can learn from him that will serve you well later in life. The rest you must discard."

If only he had. She had been right, of course, but her loving nature left them all too soon. Without her steadying hand to soothe away Andrew's bombastic nature, what had once been tolerable became unbearable. The grief they might have shared drove the wedge between them deeper. When he grabbed the belt out of Andrew's hand and turned on his father, Stephen knew he had to leave. The look of fear in his father's eyes should have made up for all of the years of healing welts that somehow reached into his soul.

Knowing he could break the man now more than twice his age brought no satisfaction to him. Getting away was his only answer. Aside from his older brother who relied on the younger brother to act as the buffer their mother had been, Stephen had no reason to stay. His brother would have to get along as best he could. What was a painful decision may well have been responsible for Andrew Angelus still being alive. Age had not improved him.

None of that was Josie's fault. His first impression of her had been way off the mark. Unlike the label of a limp-wristed helpless female he had bestowed upon her, she turned out to be a horse of an entirely different color. He had thought he knew exactly what to expect of a woman. Swallowing the knowledge he didn't have the slightest idea what made Josie tick had been a lesson in humility that still had him reeling.

Why was it he had stayed tied to the past all of this time? The answer was simple. Staying in the past gave him an excuse not to think about the future. When he held Josie while she slept, all he could think of was what might be. After so many years of convincing himself he had no capacity to share his life with anyone, how could one exasperating, captivating, impossible female change his mind so quickly? More important, how could he put a blemish-free career at risk by needing her the way he did? There weren't any answers and he missed her too much to think clearly.

Miss her? He was going crazy without her. The proper thing to do without argument was to immediately report her complete disregard for regulations to Thaddeus. That should get the old fart's head spinning. Send a rank amateur to do a professional's job? Ha. Served him right.

Walked right out the door, she did, and told me to go to hell for trying to talk some sense into her. Makes her own rules, she does. Ours aren't good enough for her. She reaches my core with no more than a touch.

Holds me. Fits me. Stirs me. Consumes me.

How long had she been gone now? It had been late afternoon when she left. It was now early morning. She should be back before long. Filling sand bags in the driving rain has got to wear thin fairly quickly. When she gets tired, she'll be ready to throw in the towel. Who am I kidding? Josie? She'd keep on filling sand bags if the whole damn valley was under water. That's the way she is. They'd find her buried in piles of mud with the freaking shovel still in her hands. Besides, I didn't encourage her to come back. I might just as well have told her to pack her bags. Why did I do that? Because I was thick enough to think I could wear her down. Am I too proud to admit I've met my match?

The blare of the phone took much longer than it should have to penetrate his one-sided dialogue. So she'd had enough, had she? He should let her stew in her own stubbornness. He grabbed the receiver.

"Having a bit of weather out there, I understand."

"Hello, Thaddeus."

"Glad, as always, to hear from me, I can tell. I was hoping we'd be able to move you directly down to LA without pausing in-between, but that may not be possible under the circumstances.

"LA?"

"Where Porter is. Have you forgotten?"

For a moment, yes he had. Such a lapse had never happened to him while on assignment. Never.

"Of course not. You know better than that."

"All I know," came the sonorous reply, "is you've spent damn near two months alone with a beautiful woman pretending to be married to her. If that doesn't distract you now and then, I can't imagine what would."

If he only knew the half of it. Get ahold of yourself, Stephen, he cautioned himself. Concentrate.

"I resent your implication," he answered as imperiously as he knew how.

"That's always been a problem with you, Angelus. Besides being totally devoid of a sense of humor, you continue to take yourself too seriously. Lighten up, why don't you?"

How could he lighten up when he was worried sick about Josie? What if she decided to take him at his word? What in the hell was he supposed to tell Thaddeus?

"So you keep telling me," he said, maintaining, he hoped, the image Thaddeus had of him. "It wouldn't be like you to call to discuss the weather, but something tells me that may be exactly what you have on your mind."

"How perceptive you are, Stephen. Satellite photos indicate the area where you are should move into a dry pattern by tonight. The only slight hitch I can see that could minimally impact you is what appears to be not much more than a stream has swollen to potential flood stage. Local authorities feel they have the situation under control if the crest doesn't go much beyond where it is right now. Given that scenario, the two of you can stay put until the end of the week. Then get set to move. We've got Porter right on the brink of being ready to fall straight into Althea's lap. Where is Josie, by the way?"

"She's, um, giving Althea a new dimension."

What the hell? Thaddeus would find out anyway.

"That sounds intriguing. Would you care to elaborate?"

"It's hard for her, Thaddeus, not to be influenced by what's going on in the area. Some of the people around these parts have had a rough go of it. Josie feels for them. Not that she hasn't done a great job, I don't mean that," he hastened to add. "She has Althea down pat."

"Now there's a departure if I've ever heard one." Thaddeus could be so snide at times. "Since when have you taken to recognizing not everyone can stay as focused as you do? Why, Stephen, you surprise me. I didn't know your unwavering resolve ever gave an inch. Exactly what is our Josie doing?"

"I'm not sure," Stephen admitted. "I tried to keep her from getting involved. We had words about it, I might add."

"I'll just bet you did."

"She swore she would stay in character."

"If she's anywhere near as good as you claim she is, I'm inclined to believe her. As a matter of fact, passing out food or whatever to storm victims might just give Althea a more credible touch in Porter's eyes."

In the interest of downplaying Josie's involvement beyond the boundaries of what Thaddeus might consider appropriate, Stephen didn't correct his false assumption. What was the point?

"She knew the risk she was taking, Thaddeus. I made that quite clear to her."

"Of that I have no doubt. So let me make this quite clear to you. Go find her immediately. Something tells me you two parted company on less than amicable terms. That is totally unacceptable. Like it or not, Stephen, she's the star of the show. I don't want any unnecessary friction between you. We can't risk having that sneak into our plans now, can we?"

"I'll get right on it," Stephen promised.

"See that you do. And Stephen?"

"Yes?"

"Apologize to her if you have to. It won't kill you."

No appropriate answer came to him. It didn't matter in any event. Thaddeus had hung up. He should take time to shave. He didn't. Even saintly Ted Hartmann could forgo a perfect image now and then. Chances were Joseph Cooper wouldn't notice. If he was home, that was.

Banging unceremoniously on Joseph's front door, Stephen let the mantle of his assumed identity settle firmly in place. It was obvious he had awakened the only person he could think of who might tell him where Josie was. Turning on effusive charm a more sophisticated recipient would have seen right through, Stephen introduced himself.

"Glad to meetcha," Joseph replied, more than graciously considering he'd probably been pulled out of a sound sleep. "What can I do for you?"

"I wondered if you could tell me where I might find my wife?" Stephen asked. "I'm worried about her."

"Fine woman, your wife," Joseph defended her.

"Yes, she is," Stephen agreed. "When did you see her last?"

"Some time yesterday if a recollect correctly." Joseph scratched his head. "She asked me to just drop her off in town, don't you know, but I could hardly do that now, could I?"

Stephen didn't see why not, but played along. "I guess not. Where did you drop her off?"

"Well, let's see. There was a command post at the Carmondys', so we went there first. Had it organized real good, they did. On account of my age, I had to allow as to how I'm not as strong as I used to be. I can remember the days when I could go on forever."

"I'm sure you can." Trying to maintain his patience wasn't easy. "You were saying about Althea?"

"Is that her name? Pretty. Never got on that familiar terms myself. I don't go in for this business of everyone calling each other by their first names right off the bat. Don't seem respectful. No young whippersnapper gets away with it with me, let me tell you."

"I'm sure they don't. Now about Althea?"

"Well, let's see. She went with the group working down by the water, I think. Would have gone myself a few years back. Never thought I'd see the day when I'd have to give in to old age."

"I'm sure they were delighted to have your help, Mr. Cooper. Where, exactly, did the group working down by the water go?"

"Oh, all over." Joseph yawned prodigiously before continuing. "You can't trust the water, you know. It's liable to gurgle up any place it darn well feels like it. Each time is different. Can't tell from one storm to the next what it's going to do."

After the unrequested litany of water related issues, the urge to choke Mr. Cooper took on epic proportions. In the interest of locating Josie, Stephen gritted his teeth instead.

"I'm sure they can't," he said. "Can you think of anyone who might have an idea with which group by wife went?"

"That's hard to say, Mr. Hartmann. Things get a little crazy when you're up against Mother Nature. Folks don't take time to introduce themselves. They just pitch in where they're needed. Of course, around here everybody pretty much knows everybody."

"I'm sure they do. That's why I thought someone might remember my wife, we being new to the area and all."

"As nice as your wife is, she's gotten to know a lot of folks, I suspect. What with her going into town and all."

Implied, but not stated, was Joseph's opinion that Mr. Hartmann was not of the same caliber as his wife. Stephen was inclined to agree with him. Before the old coot got around to nominating Josie for woman of the year, another attempt to locate her whereabouts was in order.

"You mentioned a command post," he reminded his rambling source. "Might there have been someone there keeping track of the volunteers?"

"I don't rightly know about that."

"I see. Could you direct me to the Carmondys, then? Maybe someone there could help me."

"Suit yourself. I'd go to the fire station if I was you."

"Why is that?"

"Well, that's where the main command post is."

Telling Joseph he might have mentioned that fact in the first place hardly seemed worth the breath. Stephen seized the one hopeful opening in the entire conversation, holding on for dear life.

"Good idea, Mr. Cooper." He beamed out of sheer relief at the breakthrough. "Where is the fire station?"

"In town. Right across from the grocery store," Joseph informed him as if the whole world except Stephen knew the location.

"That's a fine suggestion," Stephen said as he pumped the old man's hand. "I can't thank you enough for your help."

Getting into the car, it occurred to him he might have apologized for disturbing Mr. Cooper, or at the very least, for waking him up. Everything, including common courtesy, took a back seat to finding Josie. He had never been in town, as much from disinterest as from his habit of clinging to the shadows. Directions were unnecessary. There was only one road for him to take.

The fire station was exactly where Joseph had said it would be. Pulling into a parking place, Stephen saw that the sun had come out. He took that as a good sign. What had him stumped was how to approach whoever he encountered with a plausible excuse for having misplaced his wife. The first person Stephen saw when he got inside the station looked too tired to care.

"Help you?" the fireman asked.

"I'm Ted Hartmann," he began, "and....."

He was not allowed to finish. Tired though he evidently was, the young man in front of Stephen brightened considerably.

"If you don't mind me saying so, you've got yourself one heck of a blockbuster wife. That lady put most of the men to shame, she did. Worked like a Trojan the whole night. I don't mind telling you I didn't think she could handle a shovel, let alone know how to pick one up. I sure stand corrected."

"She's something else, all right," Stephen agreed. "Where....."

Once again he was cut off. Everyone seemed determined to draw out the process of finding Josie as long as possible, including the latest member of her fan club.

"Her stamina is something else, I tell you, and the way she encourages people? Wow. She kept telling everyone they could do just one more bag before they quit. You know what? They all did. 'Course the guys didn't want to be shown up by a woman, that's for sure. You're one lucky man, Mr. Hartmann. She's special people."

"She certainly is and I'd like to find her," he added quickly before he could get cut off again.

"That's easy," her ardent admirer said. "She's right over there."

Pointing into the central part of the building, the weary fireman indicated a cluster of cots arranged rather haphazardly around idled trucks ready for action. Josie was the only occupant, curled up on a blanket, fast asleep.

"I didn't have the heart to wake her," the man whispered. "She said she needed to rest before going home. It seemed like the least we could do."

"Thank you," Stephen said, almost abruptly, in anticipation of dismissing Althea's admirer. "I'll see to her now."

Was it his imagination or did the man hesitate ever so briefly? The clear impression he got was one of reluctance to bow out and leave them alone. The guy wasn't much past his teens, probably in his early twenties. What must he think of a man who would send his wife out into the storm to face the elements by herself? Stephen doubted Josie had mentioned him at all, leaving those around her to draw their own conclusions. The verdict was hardly in his favor.

"I'll take her home," he said, much less brusquely. "If you don't mind, I'd like to be alone with her."

Although hesitant, the man backed away, eyeing Josie's still form with a look approaching reverence. Apparently, Josie had not only helped, she had endeared Althea Hartmann to a growing number of townspeople.

"She needs the comforts of home." Stephen explained, stepping nearer to where she was. "I'm sure she's exhausted. Dry clothes, a warm bed, and large doses of TLC are definitely in order." He had reached the cot. "I'll see to it she has the best of care, believe me."

Skeptically giving up his protective stance, Josie's champion looked slightly embarrassed. Stephen felt for him.

"What is your name?" he asked.

"Marty Benson, sir."

"Well, Marty, I'm indebted to you for looking after my wife so attentively. She is, as you have found out, in a class by herself. I cheerfully admit I have trouble keeping up with her. Someday I may figure out why she married me."

He should have used that tack from the beginning. Marty Benson couldn't excuse himself fast enough. The mysteries of marriage had yet to unfold for him. Sticking around to observe whatever took place between a husband and wife was clearly out of his league.

Stephen looked down at Josie and took in the toll of her rise to local fame. She was covered with mud. Traces could be found in her hair as well as on her face. The clothes she had on were inundated. What struck him the most were her hands. Always so carefully manicured, they now bore the scars of heavy physical labor. Nails were broken, while the open palm next to her face sported a line of blisters caked in dried blood. A small bruise on her forehead marred the otherwise unblemished skin. He bent to kiss the purple colored mark. Josie opened her eyes.

"Hi," he said softly, kneeling down on the floor beside her. "You've had quite a night."

She reached out tentatively and touched his hand, gamely attempting to return his smile. As disheveled as she was, he had never seen her look more beautiful.

"I'm a bit of a mess, I'm afraid," she said in a sleep-thickened voice.

"A little soap and water will take care of that."

Turning her head into his chest, she pressed herself against him. His arms went around her. She was definitely damp and more than a little smelly. He tightened his hold.

"Ted?"

By God, she was staying in character, just as she had said she would. The final bastion of his resolve came tumbling down.

"Yes, darling?"

"Please take me home."

Chapter Ten

Was she dreaming? She must be. Warm water enveloped her like a finely spun cocoon. Careful hands had washed her, scrubbing away the filth that had permeated every pore and stretched every muscle to the breaking point. The same strong arms that had carried her, undressed her, and bathed her were still holding her. She distinctly felt his body alongside of hers. Yes, the sensation was very real indeed. Was the project still on? Who cared?

"We should get out now," he said.

"Hm."

"That wasn't the answer I was looking for, Josie. You need to be in bed."

"I'll consider it."

"Josie," his voice, though soft, took on a sterner quality, "the water will get cold."

"Then we'll add some more hot."

"You're as clean as I can get you," he said.

"One can never be too clean," she told him solemnly.

"You're getting all wrinkly. Come on, Josie. Open your eyes."

"I don't want to."

"Why?"

"Because you'll go away."

"Trust me, Josie. I'm not going anywhere. I'm not dressed for it."

"Quit being so practical. I don't want to be practical."

"Okay. If I promise not to be practical, will you get out of the tub?"

"I'll have to think about it."

No matter how real everything felt, there had to be a catch somewhere. Stephen had been crystal clear about what the consequences would be if she walked out of the door. Why hadn't he left? More than enough time had passed for him to huff and puff his way back to Thaddeus, strutting like a peacock in all his self-righteous glory. The picture was all wrong. She had defied him. He couldn't help but hate her guts.

"Josie."

"Hm?"

"I'm letting the water out of the tub."

"You'll stop at nothing to get your own way, will you?"

"I'll stop at nothing to keep you warm," he said.

Languidly twisting around toward him, she trailed her hand across the matted hair covering his chest. His arms tightened around her.

"You're supposed to be furious with me," she reminded him, testing to see what the apparition beside her would say.

"I was furious with you," he said.

Oh, dear. That didn't bode well for her.

"But you're not anymore?" she asked.

His body shifted without him changing his hold on her. The stopper of the tub released with a resounding pop.

"I should be," he told her.

"But you're not?" she repeated. Her brain wouldn't function the way she wanted it to plus her arms and legs felt like they weighed a ton.

"I tried to be, Josie."

"And?"

"It didn't work."

"That isn't at all like you, Stephen. Are you sure you've thought this through clearly?"

"Very sure."

"How confusing. I suppose you've come up with a perfectly reasonable explanation."

"I have."

"Oh good. I'll get out of this stupid tub if you'll tell me what you've so cleverly figured out."

"I've fallen in love with you."

That did it. She was dreaming. The Stephen of her dreams picked her limp body up, took her into the bedroom, and settled her on a towel to dry her off. Her mind had gone numb, of that she was sure. Whispered endearments were not part of his character. He had never said a word while he made love to her. Now, in a complete turnabout, her silent lover was telling her all sorts of unmentionable things about her eyes, her lips, and how he saw the scrawny body she thought best described as a bag of bones.

Still, as far-fetched as a flattering model of Stephen was, she rather liked listening to him. Better not to reply. If she did, the spell would be broken and the harsh realities of an utterly rash impulse on her part would loom up to haunt her. Stephen in love with her? Wouldn't that be a fine how-de-do?

Rather than a list of incriminations concerning her rushing into the swirling midst of a disaster operation about which she knew nothing, she was being soothed in the most fanciful way. How she wanted to believe what she knew she couldn't be hearing. What was the harm in pretending, just for now, that he cared for her in the same way she had begun to care for him? The piper would need to be paid soon enough. When that time came, her only hope of having a fighting chance against him depended on a position of strength. At the moment, she was as weak as a kitten. After a short rest, filled with wild imaginings, she'd take on Stephen Angelus with her usual vigor.

The next thing she became aware of was a hideous smell invading her idyllic refuge where she was hiding. Before she could pinpoint what the odor was, her rubbery legs were receiving such exquisite attention, whatever the stink was took a back seat to the kneading fingers massaging away the pain. Feeling amazingly refreshed, she chanced taking a peek at the action. So engrossed in his administrations, he was not aware of being watched, she could look at her man of many talents with guarded eyes. She had never seen him frown.

"What's wrong?" she asked.

"You're awake," he observed.

"I think I am," she replied, more than a little unsure of how to proceed. "That feels good."

"I'm surprised you have any feeling at all."

"If wretched agony counts, I'd say my nerve endings are charging away on all cylinders."

"I suspected as much. Sorry this liniment smells to high heaven. Its redeeming feature is it works miracles."

His hands never stopped as he spoke. Sure she was awake now, how to behave herself properly with the new improved version of Stephen wasn't coming through loud and clear. Perhaps facing the music head on was the best approach.

"A miracle may be just what I need right now," she said. "Did I blow the whole shebang entirely?"

His hands stopped. Here came the dreaded explosion.

"No."

That was it. Nothing more. His hands began to move again.

"What do you mean, no?"

Controlling her voice, which had taken on a slightly hysterical edge, didn't seem necessary. What a way to extract his revenge. Whether she liked it or not, she was going to have to go digging for an explanation. To her way of thinking, she'd done all the digging she ever planned to do in her whole life. What other choice did she have?

"Could you please explain what you mean?" she asked as humbly as she knew how.

He sat back on his heels and looked down at her. Instead of the avenging angel she expected, he had the audacity to look like a charming rogue. Here was the man she had dreamed said he was in love with her. Instead of concentrating on feeling contrite, she couldn't help thinking how much she wanted to bear his children, so long as they all looked like him.

"What you did, Josie, was another one of your strokes of genius."

"Excuse me? If you want my description of my most recent escapade, harebrained lunacy has a whole new meaning. I should have stopped and thought first instead of charging out of here like some Joan of Arc type bent on saving the world."

"That may be what you thought you were doing, more in retaliation to me, I think, than because you had a burning desire to lead the local sandbag brigade. We were both way off base, Josie. I should have let go of my sense of superiority, but I didn't know how until I faced what life was like without you. There was a genuine need for help and you used it to get my dander up. How little either of us knew you'd be supplying the folks back in Washington with exactly the legitimacy they were seeking. The Hartmanns now have a verifiable existence, thanks to you. To say nothing of the fact if you ran for mayor tomorrow, you'd be a shoo-in."

The words, although understood, didn't register. Was he actually praising her?

"That's ridiculous," she stammered. "I hurt all over, I had no more call to be out playing cheerleader than you had to keep hammering on me, and what do you mean, running for mayor?"

"You won their hearts, Josie, as only you can. They may think it was Althea that urged them on, but I know it was that indomitable spirit of yours. I couldn't break it. Lord knows I tried."

"I told you from the very beginning my mind was made up," she told him. "You only did what you thought was right. You weren't exactly thrilled at the prospect of me walking into your well-ordered career, wreaking havoc along the way."

His hands went back to massaging her legs. The spreading warmth reached up her thighs of its own accord.

"On the contrary, Josie, you were exactly what I needed. I just didn't know it."

"You needed me?" she asked incredulously. "All I seem to do is upset your apple cart."

"Among other things. All my life I've had a stubborn streak a mile wide. I should have gotten rid of it a long time ago, but I carried it around as an excuse not to get close to people. It worked real well until I met you."

"Me?"

"Yep."

"What did I do?"

"You didn't play by my rules. That threw me off."

"I couldn't play by your rules," she reminded him, "because you wouldn't tell me what they were."

"It was my only defense against letting you in, don't you see? From the get-go I wanted the one thing I didn't dare risk having, Josie."

"Which was?"

"You."

Now she was really puzzled. "But you did have me, Stephen, whenever you wanted me, in as willing a way as I knew how to be. That's what confuses me so much. Maybe I missed the finer points of a relationship along the way. In bed, I thought you cared. Out of it, you kept turning away from me."

"Because I wasn't playing by the rules either, Josie. Not mine, but the ones that kept me alive in this crazy business I call an occupation. What was worse, in my eyes, was I couldn't stop myself. I looked at that as a weakness, something I would conquer as time went by. The only problem was, I didn't want to stop. I wanted more. I wanted what I had convinced myself I would never have. It scared the shit out of me."

Ignoring her groaning muscles, Josie pushed herself up on her elbows. So he had been having thoughts very similar to hers. No wonder he'd been such a pill at times. That, she knew, was only part of it. There had been a woman in his life who had soured him. She knew the feeling all too well.

"Whoever hurt you did a bang-up job," she told him, "and it wasn't your father. Who was she?"

Seeing the pain cross his face, she reached out to him. He took her hand and raised it to his lips.

"I've called her many things," he said. "The term gold digger is the one reserved for polite society. The list of excuses for not seeing what she was is endless. The fact remains I didn't want to see what she was. What I saw was a very pretty, very willing lady of what my father called Southern quality who thought I was the hottest ticket to hit the face of the earth."

"I'm sure you were," Josie said.

"At eighteen, every man thinks he's a stud waiting for a happening. In my case, all I needed was the slightest encouragement. What I got was an all-out attack."

"Do tell me about this vision of loveliness with a heart of stone," she said.

"Ah, but there you are in error. Vivian has no heart. Her driving force is naked ambition fueled by pure greed. She's got a trail of I think it's four ex-husbands to prove it. As a young girl, she had at least what I suppose might have been an acceptable excuse."

"Which was?"

"An old family name requiring a significant shot of cold hard cash to cover up years of decay. Without any guarantee of a reversal of fortune, Vivian set out to rectify the matter single handedly."

"So she went husband hunting?"

"More or less. Anyone would do. I happened to be handy."

"And if I'm not mistaken," Josie guessed, "not all that familiar with the fairer sex."

"A babe in the woods," Stephen admitted. "There was my mother, of course, but as close as we were, regarding some subjects she might have helped me with, I was too embarrassed to ask. Going to my father was out of the question. He would have laughed in my face. So, all I had to go on was a rather pathetic array of misconceptions I had collected from porn books and woefully uninformed friends. You can be sure Vivian knew exactly what my limitations were."

Josie could easily imagine the way Stephen had been back then. Gone was the careful veneer he always kept in place. He looked younger when he relaxed, exposing carefully hidden emotions for her to see. She wanted to tell him that what happened with Vivian didn't matter, and she would have, except she could see he wanted to tell her about it.

"The Baldwin lands, at one time, adjoined ours. To pay off debts, Vivian's father had sold off portions over the years, always refusing any offer my father made. That act in itself endeared me to Mr. Baldwin. I had no way of knowing what my father offered amounted to less than pennies on the dollar. All I knew was the Baldwins were neighbors, part of the scenery I took for granted. By the time I was eighteen, the family fortune had been frittered away, a fact not generally known, especially not by the younger crowd. When Vivian went into action, I wouldn't have cared if the family was literally down to rubbing two pennies together. You are aware, I'm sure," he leaned toward her to emphasize his point, "such thinking is heresy in the blue-blooded world of the horsey set."

"I'm sure it is," she replied.

"It's funny," he reflected, "Vivian didn't really stand out as a kid. She was just sort of there. As soon as her hormones got into the action, however, she sure filled out in spectacular fashion. Armed with her new potent ammunition, she went into high gear. I never saw what was coming. She flirted. She teased. She promised and once she had me dangling, she reneged. I never stopped to think she had any ulterior motive other than she found me irresistible."

"When in doubt," Josie said, "flatter the male ego."

"That wasn't all she flattered. Looking back on it, I'm really galled I could have been so stupid. There I was thinking I could give Casanova a pointer or two while Vivian was avidly convincing she had never been so satisfied. Had she been more practiced, she might have pulled it off. What in reality were lapses wide enough to drive a truck through, I started to see as hairline fractures I couldn't ignore as hard as I tried."

"Such as?"

"Minute details, really, that she hadn't memorized as well as she thought she had. Her biggest mistake was not keeping to what she knew best. Thinking an interest in our stable operations would show how attracted she was to me, her vain attempts at engaging in anything approaching a meaningful equestrian discussion fell flat. After constantly correcting her, hooked though I may have been, I finally caught on. What I didn't do, which I should have done, was dump her right then and there. Instead I made excuses, refusing to see her for what she was. The result, of course, is I made a royal ass of myself."

"The first person in the world to ever do so," she teased, gently squeezing his hand. "Do you think I'm proud of what I got into with Jason?"

He evidently had not expected her to make the comparison. Always self-contained, he must have started building the shell so long ago because he was ashamed of being taken in. Funny, she had often been embarrassed by what had happened with Jason, but never ashamed.

"When you grow up as insulated as I was," he told her, looking down at their entwined fingers, "you don't accept a serious brush with exposure."

"Did you think you were immune?" she asked.

"I probably did," he admitted, "at least as far as a feminine antagonist was concerned. Without any thoughts of chauvinism, believe me. Vivian planted a poison and I never gave myself the chance to find out one flavor does not a menu make."

"But you're such a good lover," she blurted out before she could stop herself. "How could you hate women and be so good at pleasing them?"

Uncomfortable didn't really describe his expression. A better description would fall somewhere between him facing the unfamiliar or warily treading into unchartered waters. Rather than look away from him after her outburst, she watched him intently.

"You did that," he said haltingly.

"You're kidding."

"Not by a long shot."

"I don't understand," she told him. "From the first time you held me, it was as if you knew every secret desire I've ever had."

"No, Josie, that's not it."

"Then, what?"

"You are the kind of woman who deserves to be aroused slowly. In doing so, I found I increased my own responses. I didn't think any woman could do that to me."

He was serious. It was her turn to flounder. The last thing she expected of Stephen Angelus was a confession of how he felt about making love to her. She sank back against the pillows, totally forgetting about how much she hurt all over. No liniment made had the same effect as the slow heat spreading through her.

"I think I'd like to hear more about that," she said, reaching out to turn his face back to hers.

"You're not like any woman I've ever met before." His eyes searched hers for acceptance of what he had said.

"Maybe next time you'll choose your seat more carefully," she said. "I've been told transatlantic flights are a hot bed of boy meets girl situations."

"We didn't meet by chance, Josie. It was all a set-up from the very beginning." Seeing her surprise, he explained further. "I didn't know any more than you did until Thaddeus started quizzing me about my trip back to the states. He looked inordinately pleased when I told him I had sat by a woman whom I found damn attractive."

"You should have asked to have your seat changed," she said weakly, still digesting how long an arm Thaddeus had. "Think of the aggravation you would have saved yourself."

His smile was positively illegal. No man had the right to melt her heart the way he did.

"One could well say that about you too," he said, inching his way across the bed until he fit against her body. "I guess it could be said you got so good at aggravating me I couldn't do anything else except admit that I loved you."

She knew she wasn't dreaming this time. Stephen had definitely said he loved her. Speechless, she turned to him.

"I know," he said, "what a revolting development that is. Right?"

"No," she stammered, "not at all. Not very timely perhaps, but never revolting."

"At least it puts us on a level playing field," he said with a grin.

"How's that?" she asked, brushing her nose against his.

"I've never done an assignment under these circumstances, so we both get a crack at seeing how well we carry it off."

So he thought she was referring to the project as a stumbling block to time. Maybe it was better that he didn't know all of the gory details about the mess Jason had left her in. A woman with as much liability as she had might easily make Vivian look like a piker.

"Why would that be a problem?" she asked as if she didn't know. "Aren't we supposed to be married?"

"The operative words there are supposed to be, Josie. When you're pretending, it's easy to be detached. Caring about someone can cloud your judgment, leading to less than optimum results."

Somehow, results, optimum or otherwise, seemed very far away with him next to her. That was probably his point. Being a little short in the optimum department, what else could she hope to have with him? Love of the lasting variety couldn't be under the circumstances. She'd take what she could get and face the consequences later.

"After what we've been through so far," she informed him, "a new twist on things just might push us up to a higher level."

"We'll find out together," he replied, drawing her closer to him.

"Sounds good to me," she told him, giving herself over to the anticipation of what she read in his eyes.

A sudden thought completely wrecked her mood. Sitting bolt upright, she turned to the startled figure bedside her.

"What's the matter?" he asked.

"The water, Stephen."

"What about it?"

"Did we stop it?"

She had never seen him crack up. How could he be laughing that hard when her intentions had been so good? Had she put herself through the hardest thing she had ever done in her life for nothing?

"Well?" she demanded, grabbing his arms, trying to get him to stop laughing so he could talk to her.

"Yes," he finally managed to gasp out between gulping chuckles. Pulling her back into his arms, he held her until the last giggle subsided. "You may have sore muscles for a week and God only knows when your hands will recover, but you sure as hell kept your finger in the dike."

"This is good," she said, giggling back at him in spite of herself. "Now that I've settled that, where were we?"

"I was thinking of ravishing you," he answered, picking her up and settling her on top of himself.

"Slowly?" she asked, delighting in the hardness of him beneath her.

"But of course," he assured her before covering her mouth with his.

And he proceeded to do so.

Chapter Eleven

❖

If he had been a betting man, Stephen would have put money on a slow recovery for his fair-skinned Josie. True to her unpredictable nature, she proved him wrong. Whether it was pure tenacity or the sobering realization their days in the mountain house were numbered, he couldn't be sure. As familiar as he was with the art of disguise, it had never occurred to him one trip to a beauty salon, complete with a talented manicurist, could make such a difference. Along with her nail repair, the ever-amazing Althea made the directed hair style change and started wearing tinted contacts to minimize the impact of her eyes.

Only the healing blisters on her hands remained as a memorial to what they referred to as the sand bag caper. Unless, of course, he counted the ever-present trail of admirers paying court to the local heroine. Much to his amusement, Josie could hardly be described as a willing recipient of fawning admiration.

"It's totally embarrassing," she fumed, hunkering down in the front seat of the car as he pulled out of the grocery store parking lot. "You could have at least gone in with me to help fend off the attackers."

"Not on your life," he replied.

"You're really enjoying this, aren't you?" Her feathers were definitely ruffled.

"Enjoying isn't exactly how I'd describe my feelings," he told her. "I think I'm intrigued more than anything else by your modesty. It's a side of you I wasn't aware you had."

The set of her jaw said she could just as well have kept it hidden. "Well, I'm not going to the store anymore," she declared stoutly. "That way you won't be able to extract your revenge so cleverly."

"Revenge?" he asked

"You don't fool me, Stephen." She was genuinely pissed. He wasn't quite sure why. "Deep down, you're still of the opinion I should have listened to you and behaved myself." Ah, so that was it. "Seeing me squirm must be giving you more satisfaction than you care to let on."

"That's not true," he defended himself. "What you did took a lot of nerve and I admire that."

"It took a lot of nerve to foolishly barge into something I had no business doing or it took a lot of nerve to defy you?" she asked.

"Both, I suppose, but I needed to be taken down a peg or two as hard as it is for me to admit." Josie glanced at him skeptically. "I mean it," he assured her. "You called it right when you said I never allowed for compassion. It's high time I corrected that and viewed the world a lot less jadedly."

Straightening up from her slouched position, she looked at him sideways. Her face had softened considerably.

"Maybe for the time being you shouldn't consider playing the knight in shining armor," she said. "One of us has to keep this operation on track."

"I liked your hair better the other way," he said, not yet ready to go back to the job he knew he was supposed to do.

"It's hardly any different at all," she replied, raising her hand to touch her hair self-consciously.

"It's very different to me," he insisted. "This style says don't touch me. The way you wear your hair doesn't say that."

The blush crept slowly across her face. She turned away from him. As strange as it seemed, the woman who had won him over was sometimes almost shy with him. It stood to reason. When he stopped to think about their situation, they hardly knew each other really. When they made love, they were in total harmony. Otherwise, they were feeling their way along rather gingerly. He reached out and put his arm across her shoulders. She turned back to him. The captivating blush was gone.

"You say some of the weirdest things," she told him. "I don't know why they affect me the way they do."

"I don't know either, Josie, but I like the effect. Would I be right if I guessed you're not all that used to having someone comment about intimate incidentals?"

The shrug of her shoulders was hardly a movement at all. She bit her lower lip before answering.

"Actually, I guess I'm not. I think what's really getting to me now is the change in you. Not that I'm complaining," she added quickly. "It's just I had gotten so used to being on my guard with you. Oh, what the heck. You're right. I'm not very used to going below the surface. I haven't had much time to practice. The only person in my life so far who lets it all hang out is Rosemary."

"Didn't she raise you?" he asked.

Her eyebrows went up. "Rosemary? Heavens no. My exposure to her was kept to a strict minimum."

"By whom?"

"By Aunt Minerva," she replied as if everyone in the world knew who Aunt Minerva was.

"Okay," he said, "I'll bite. Who is Aunt Minerva?"

"She was my father's sister," Josie explained. "When Mama died, my father thought she would be a better influence on me than Rosemary. From what I can surmise, he didn't approve of my godmother. I think the only reason he went along with my mother's choice was because she wouldn't hear any arguments against her best friend, as odd a relationship as theirs was."

"How so?"

"My mother, as best I can figure out, was the exact opposite of Rosemary with one exception. They both believed in absolute loyalty no matter what. They grew up together as friends and vowed to stay that way. That's just what they did up to the last minute. If it hadn't been for Rosemary, Mama would have died alone."

"How old were you?" he asked.

"Seven," she answered. "My grasp on the concept of death wasn't real sharp at that point. Rosemary did her best to help me understand, but she didn't stay around long enough to get me over the hump. My father wanted her gone and made no bones about it. Maybe he felt guilty about not being next to his wife when she died. Somehow I doubt it. His one concession was I could spend two weeks each year with Rosemary and Wendall. At all other times, I was under Aunt Minerva's watchful eyes.

"She wasn't a bad sort, really. Her basic failing was a complete ignorance of children. I was properly fed and decently clothed. Period. I quickly learned avoiding Aunt Minerva was to my advantage. Not that she ever abused me. She didn't. Her idea of guiding my development consisted of a million homilies all involving things I wasn't to do. As far as I could tell, there wasn't a permissible action available to me. Put that up against Rosemary's liberal ideas and you get one real confused kid. I sometimes wonder how I would have turned out had fate not intervened big time."

"Meaning?" he asked, fascinated by her account.

"My father and Aunt Minerva were killed in a freak accident when I was seventeen. With no one left to interfere, Rosemary took charge as only she can. Her knowledge of human limitations is amazing. She knew darn well my view of the world was a tad skewed. As much as possible, my eyes were opened gradually. I owe her my college education and the range of opportunities she opened to me. I wish I had used them better. The one hurdle that's so hard to get over is that group of beliefs drummed into me day after day as a child."

"Such as?" he urged her to continue.

"A list of don'ts a mile wide a true lady adheres to at all times," she intoned with all the emphasis of a revival preacher.

He pulled the car into the driveway, stopping in front of the house. "Do any of them cover the opposite sex?" he asked.

Josie did a super impression of a dyed-in-the wool prude. "Some subjects we simply do not discuss," she replied tartly. "Modesty forbids it."

"And of course anything approaching a compliment must never be allowed to go to our heads," he guessed.

"Compliments," she informed him, "are the devil's way of leading us into purgatory. How we look or what kind of impression we make is immaterial. Anyone who feels the need to comment is insincere and should be ignored."

He reached over and drew her into his arms. "You are beautiful," he said, breathing into the hairdo he didn't like, "even with all these changes I wish you didn't have to make. I'm glad you're not Althea."

"Oh, but I am," she assured him.

"Always?" he teased.

"Well, not always." She squirmed slightly from his deep look into her eyes. "That would be impossible."

"Tell me when you're not Althea," he insisted, letting his lips hover just above hers.

"Like now."

He was toast. Reaching behind his head, she curled her fingers into the hair as the base of his neck while her tongue teased at his lips to be allowed in. The taste of her filled him. Like him, she spoke best when she didn't speak at all. Pulling back slowly, he looked down at her.

"When we first came here, I think we could have safely stripped and had at it. Now, with your fan club flitting onto the scene at odd moments, I'm not so sure."

She stuck out her tongue at him and opened the car door. "I'm not amused," she threw back at him, "and I most certainly am not beautiful."

He caught her hand before she could get away from him. "You are to me," he told her. "Aunt Minerva had it all wrong." Josie looked uncomfortable. "Don't tell me no one has never told you you're pretty. Very pretty."

A guarded expression crossed over her face. She'd been told all right. Many times. It was entirely possible Jason had told her quite often. That might explain why she was dubious.

"I believe you think I am," she said slowly. "The other people don't matter."

He let go of her hand to let her escape into the house. Some women used their beauty much in the way Aunt Minerva had probably had in mind when she cautioned the young girl she knew was exceptional. Vivian still traded on her looks neither time nor a string of husbands had destroyed. Yet. The years had a way of taking their toll. Josie had the type of beauty that he felt sure would stretch into old age. He had every intention of being around to see if he was right. Going to the trunk of the car for the bags of groceries, he then went toward the front door.

Before he reached the steps, Josie filled the door frame looking more than a little rattled. Without having to ask, he knew why she looked the way she did.

"Is it show time?" he asked.

"Almost," she answered. "We are to be ready to leave the day after tomorrow."

"Well, that takes care of you having to go back to the grocery store," he said, going around her and into the kitchen. "What's the schedule?"

"I have it here," she replied, following along behind him. "Darn you for insisting we always check faxes and messages before anything else. I was just beginning to get my good humor back. Why a private plane?"

"Image is everything, my dear." He ignored her good humor remark. "The Hartmanns have money to burn. Why shouldn't they have a plane?"

"How big is it?"

Her aversion to flying came back to him. "It will be top of the line, I'm sure. At any rate, it's a short flight."

"All that means is the take-off and landing are closer together," she pointed out. "Couldn't we drive?"

"So I detect cold feet?" he asked.

"You know perfectly well I'm nowhere near as confident as I'd like to be. How can you always be so sure of yourself?"

Honesty never hurt. Especially now when Josie needed all of the assurance she could get.

"I'm not as confident as you give me credit for being," he confessed. "I get butterflies every time. Anyone who doesn't probably isn't going to last very long in this business. A good set of controlled nerves keeps a person sharp."

"Either that or drives a lesser fool to an early grave," she observed.

"I take that very personally," he told her, feigning indignation. "I trained you. Remember?"

Her look of desperation started to fade. The fighter in her took over.

"You're right, I'm sure," she said, trying her best to look confident. "I'd feel a lot better if we didn't have to fly though."

"Now, come on," he cajoled, putting his hand under her pouting chin. "You've faced a lot worse than a plane ride with more guts than most. If it will make you feel any better, we can hide away in the privacy of the sleeping quarters and screw the whole trip."

Her eyes widened. "You mean there's a bedroom?"

"Of some sort I would guess. You insist on the best, Mrs. Hartmann."

"Wouldn't the pilot know what we were doing?"

"He could probably figure it out."

"I'd be mortified." Aunt Minerva's teachings, no doubt. "What else do you suggest?"

"Making the best of the amenities before you have to watch every move you make," he suggested, drawing her against the hardness quickly reacting to his talk of making love.

"Anything else?"

Grinding against him, she openly showed how receptive she was to his preamble.

"I think you've found the key," he replied, hungrily taking possession of her mouth.

The need he had for her blocked out every caution he normally took to slow his pace down. More than raw lust drove him. A protective surge took over, forcing him to face a conclusion to the mission he had never had to consider in the past. For himself, he accepted the dangers. Applying the same guidelines to Josie was impossible. They couldn't go back now. It was too late. Somehow he had to master the capacity to look out for her while at the same time doing his damnedest to remain as aloof as possible. Could he do it? What other choice did he have?

As if she realized the urgency pressing him on, Josie matched his momentum with equal abandon. Totally unconcerned with anything other than satisfying the powerful craving to be lost in each other, they didn't bother with any pretense of finesse. Roughly uncovering them both, he pushed into her without preliminaries. She was thoroughly ready, grasping at him to bury his solid heat as deeply as he could. Each thrust was more compelling than the one before. They were locked in a frenzy of reaching a completion fed solely by undisguised passion. Vaguely aware she would bruise from the impact of his exploration over the soft flesh of her throat, he couldn't stop himself. His fingers dug into her buttocks as he guided the frantic rhythm consuming them.

She uttered a cry of success when her climax started, shuddering against him as the full impact hit her. Keeping his own climax at bay for as long as he possibly could served to increase the fierce intensity that rocked his body. They clung to each other. Merged totally, neither was inclined to let go. In that moment of complete union, he got the sense Josie knew as well as he their love making, along with everything else in their lives, would be relegated to a secondary position until the mission was completed. And then? He couldn't think about that. He was having enough trouble coping as it was with what he had gotten himself into. Formulating a future was one stumbling block he wasn't prepared to contemplate. Josie stirred in his arms and looked up at him.

"Can we get Porter, Stephen?"

Still infused with the flush of his stimulation, she was every inch the woman he had always wanted. Ready or not, their course was set.

"If we don't," told her, "we're in a heap of trouble."

"Well," she declared, sticking her chin out confidently, "we can't have that, can we?"

The inner strength she had developed to cope with life sustained her better than any encouragement he might have given her. He had no doubt she was any less scared. Having allowed her fit of nerves to show, she took hold of herself just like she had during the initial phase of her training. When they left the house for the airport, Althea Hartmann was firmly in place, not showing a flicker of the dread she had toward the flight ahead of her.

Thaddeus had outdone himself. The limousine sent to meet them at the appointed spot several miles from the airport served as a perfect indication of the upcoming luxury that was to surround them. Uneasy though she probably was, even Josie had to be impressed by the plush appointments of the sleek little jet that was their transportation to Los Angeles. Once inside, the atmosphere had nothing in common with the compressed aspects of commercial liners. Althea Hartmann took each feature in without any sign of being affected one way or the other, including the separate sleeping quarters with oversized lounge chairs to serve as beds.

"We must see about a more functional arrangement in there," she remarked enigmatically.

Only the slightest twinkle in her eyes as she looked at Stephen gave any indication of a totally different meaning than she had expressed. At that moment, he realized the mission was on rock solid ground. What he had considered to be a thoroughly ill-advised gamble had turned out to be golden and it was all because of a persevering female who refused to be beaten.

Of all the people he had trained over the years, she was the first he would get to see in action. To be more precise, she was the only one he had ever cared to see in action. Better still, they were in the thick of things together, both depending on the other to survive. The realization he could put his trust in her should have shaken him to the core. Instead, he found the phenomenon positively invigorating.

The agent assigned to act as the attendant on the flight probably thought they held hands throughout the trip to sustain the illusion of a happily married couple. After all, everyone at Keener & Cooke, Inc. knew Stephen Angelus had a full size freezer in the place where his heart was supposed to be.

Making a comparison between the mountain house and the gated mansion secluded away in an exclusive LA enclave favored by the rich and famous boggled the imagination. The stripped down utilitarian training facility sported bare essentials. Its one redeeming feature was the imposing view. Every unnecessary gizmo known to man had a niche somewhere in their new location. Designed purely for show, each room was perfectly arranged, eliminating any pretense of comfort. Surface people like the Hartmanns ranked those with whom they associated by their possessions. Stephen had known too many of them, avoiding their ilk whenever possible. In all probability, every expansive window in the house commanded a spectacular view, including the city of Los Angeles spread out below. With the ever present smog hanging low over the entire area, the view, like the house, was devoid of any character.

Barred from lifting a finger to help with the unpacking process, Stephen and Josie played their roles by sitting out in the hazy sunshine next to the pool.

The staff required to support the picture they wanted to present was a mixture of agency personnel sprinkled among those hired from the local area. After so many weeks of having privacy assured, an arrangement discouraging breaking out of character for fear of blowing the whole sham made him uncomfortable for the first time in his career. Taking stock, he realized being under the scrutiny of others was much more to his advantage. Like it or not, he was forced to stifle the urge to concern himself with Josie's feelings. From the look of her, she gave no indication she needed any help from him at all.

"We'll need to find a good decorator," Althea declared, stifling a yawn.

Unsure of which direction she was taking, Stephen simply looked over at her with an encouraging, "oh?"

"Most certainly. We will need to give this place our own personality."

"What's wrong with it?" he asked, knowing exactly what she was saying.

"Honestly, Ted, you men have no flair whatsoever. Nothing's wrong with it except the colors are all off, the furniture has no period focus, and whoever picked out the drapes must have specialized is a mass produced hotel approach. I was thinking of a more sedate look. What do you think?"

"Whatever you want, my dear," the dutiful husband replied, going back to his newspaper.

He didn't need to look at her to know the snug little smile Josie had made a part of Althea was firmly in place. Women like Althea expected to get their own way. It was a mystery to him why they didn't just go ahead and do what they wanted to do. Instead, there was always the ritual of a consensus-gathering tactic. Where Josie had learned about that, he didn't know unless Rosemary had shown her the way.

At any rate, the tidbit of conversation was as good as any for their audience carefully busying themselves with cleaning the patio furniture. Althea would treat servants as invisible objects, no less completely aware of their presence. Having grown up in such an atmosphere, Stephen knew the ropes without ever having been specifically told. Josie had needed to learn by observation.

Waiting for the anticipated meeting with Porter Holloway was made more tedious by the precious few hours they could snatch for themselves. Always on edge when the main event was close at hand, Stephen felt himself being wound tighter and tighter, passing the time in carefully orchestrated groundwork set-ups staged for Porter's benefit. He hid his impatience brilliantly when they were on display. Alone with Josie, he let it all hang out.

"I thought you said these frivolous little escapades were necessary," Josie said, shedding Althea as soon as they could escape to the large master suite.

"They are," he agreed sourly. "We can't expect to waltz up to him without a proper basis of believability. Overpriced food and painfully lacking talent get to me, that's all."

Leaning over to remove her contacts, Josie was visibly more relaxed than he. In his current frame of mind, her ability to bear up so well only added to his frustration.

"Rodeo Drive was kind of fun," she observed.

"Everything we do now is window dressing." Rodeo Drive had been a royal pain.

He sat down heavily on the end of the oversized king bed. Even the bed annoyed him. It was too damn big.

"This is the hardest part for you, isn't it, Stephen?" She sat down beside him.

"Yes," he admitted. "When you've done everything you can do, it's time to get on with things."

"I can't imagine it will be too much longer," she said. "Porter is in no position to be coy if he wants to be king of the missiles game. How many years did you say the government has been making huge contributions in the Hartmann's name?"

"Four, I think."

"Aside from the terrible waste of taxpayers' money, don't you think Uncle Sam wants a return on his investment? We're their ace in the hole, but there ain't no way a good poker player hurries the action," Josie said.

"Why do I get the idea our roles have suddenly reversed?" he asked.

Her disquieting violet eyes looked at him closely. "Isn't that the way it's supposed to be sometimes, Stephen? I mean, no one expects you to be the big tough guy all of the time."

"Nobody except me," he groused, catching her slender wrists in his hands. "How can I expect to maintain my stud reputation otherwise?"

She fell on top of him, flattening them on the brocade bedspread. Her perfume intoxicated him as he ran his hands over the smoothness of her skin. A discreet knock on the door quickly put an end to his exploration.

"Timing is everything," she whispered, scrambling off of the bed. "I think I'll disappear."

As soon as she slipped into her dressing room, Stephen asked who was at the door. The rather stuffy agent, Arthur Grimes, with whom he had worked before, announced himself in his assumed role as a sort of glorified butler.

"Come in," Stephen said curtly.

"Sorry to bother you, sir, but you have a phone call."

"Who is it?" Stephen asked.

"Someone by the name of Porter Holloway, sir."

The reason Grimes had never risen higher in the ranks than he had was his inability to control his face. He looked about to burst. Had he known what he had interrupted, he probably would have.

"I'll take it."

Dismissing Grimes with a wave of his hand, Stephen picked up the receiver. From all indications, the man who introduced himself could easily have been the sincere crusader he presented himself to be. Of all possible scenarios put forth to set up their initial contact, having Porter make the first move was considered the most ideal. His eagerness to meet the Hartmanns bolstered their credibility. Claiming prior commitments until Porter suggested they might like to attend an informal get-together at what he modestly referred to as his humble home, Stephen controlled the arrangements to agency specifications.

Porter invited only the most elite to his home, a surprisingly large group. In such an environment, the Hartmanns would blend in while at the same time sparing themselves the undue attentiveness of their host. Bait was always much more tantalizing when dangled just out of reach.

Before Porter could attempt to ingratiate himself further, Stephen eased out of the conversation oozing Southern charm. The image of a conniving schemer licking his chops in anticipation of getting one step closer to being the munitions king of the world immediately came to mind. The investment of time and sacrifice was so close to paying off, Porter was probably headed straight for the liquor cabinet. Let him celebrate. He'd have the rest of his life to contemplate how the best laid plans slipped through his fingers. After Althea Hartmann got through with him, he might welcome an uninterrupted stretch of time to recover.

The house was far from humble. Giving his riches away to the poor was not among Porter's repertoire of selected charitable endeavors. During the drive from their home, conversation had no part in the short ride. Conversation would have been distracting. Each used the time to sink fully into their roles, he from habit, she as the result of his careful training. When deposited at Porter's front door, the metamorphosis was complete. Althea was the star. Ted couldn't have been happier basking in her reflected glory.

Porter's reaction to his intended mark had certain similarities to those of the other men close by when Althea swept through the door. She didn't enter the house. She descended upon it.

Something akin to jealousy tried to distract Stephen momentarily. Control returned to him quickly. The same could not be said for Porter. Cleverly made up and dressed to capture the essence of the fine line between proper and too revealing, Althea commanded attention.

Allowing her host to hold her hand a fraction of a second too long for propriety, she created the distinct impression the lapse was entirely his. The criminal posing as a devout Christian temporarily lost control of his dulcet tones as he collected himself. Clearing his throat several times eliminated the quavering timbre of a bagpipe slowly losing air as he passed among his guests to introduce the Hartmanns.

Those in attendance had been thoroughly researched to eliminate any unnecessary surprises. A few had achieved a name for themselves as entertainers. Most were successful professionals used to giving a certain amount of time to chosen charitable causes. Several were influential legislators.

Porter had studied his audience well. They were not gullible. He counted on the sincerity of their beliefs to achieve his ends. How they would react to his deception wasn't clear. Devout or not, in Stephen's experience forgiveness came easier to some than to others. There was a certain measure of satisfaction to be had from helping the process of assuring Porter's downfall.

Recognizing such an emotion came as a jolt. Never, as far as he could recall, had Stephen ever taken ownership of his cases. Once completed, the job was forgotten. Thaddeus had ripped the rug out from under him by changing the rules. How intentional his motives were was open to speculation. The creation of Althea Hartmann had been carefully crafted. Now he could watch the results of what had been the hardest weeks of his life along with the most confusing.

While Althea flattered and fawned over their salivating host, Stephen searched the crowd looking for the agent who had infiltrated Porter's inner circle. He and another man were standing beside the huge grand piano dominating the expansive area beyond the foyer. Pretending to have an interest in the impressive instrument, Stephen couldn't believe his luck. The other man was Porter's most trusted associate, Elijah Flude, a convicted felon who claimed to have found Jesus while in prison. That sham, no doubt, had been orchestrated by Porter. The closest Elijah had ever gotten to Jesus was walking by a crèche display during the Christmas holidays.

"Mr. Hartmann," the agent said, moving toward Stephen, "I'm Jonah Marteen, and this is Elijah Flude."

Shaking hands first with Elijah before turning his attention to the man purporting to be Jonah allowed the smooth exchange of a small cassette to pass between them. It was quickly stowed away out of sight.

"Please call me Ted," Stephen said to both men. "It's a pleasure meeting both of you. It must be very gratifying for you to work with a man like Porter."

"He's an inspiration to us all," Elijah intoned with about as much conviction as the Pope announcing he had embraced homosexuality. "I must admire your beautiful wife, Ted. She's one fine looking woman."

"Well, thank you, Elijah." He had an opening and lost no time taking advantage of it. "I hate to admit it, but she's almost more than I can handle."

"Is that so?" Jonah helped him along.

"Are either of you married?" They both shook their heads. "Then you have no idea what a woman can be like when she wants a baby. It should be heaven on earth, but she's at me constantly to do my duty as she calls it."

Elijah rolled his eyes, clearly thinking were the roles reversed, he'd be more than up to the task. "How often we talkin' about. Ted?"

"I swear she'd be at it ten times a day if it were possible," Stephen improvised. "Now, don't get me wrong. I'm as committed to having a child as she is. I just think she's a bit over-zealous."

The wheels were churning so fast in Elijah's head, they were almost audible. What better news could he give to Porter than the latest mark was hornier than a bitch in heat? Stephen decided to let him spread the news as quickly as possible.

"As a matter of fact," he looked at his watch, "I promised I'd let her know when we were half an hour away from the optimum temperature time. It was nice meeting both of you. Excuse me."

Elijah barely said good-bye, taking off toward Porter literally rubbing his palms together. Jonah gave a thumbs up sign before blending in with the rest of the crowd, leaving Stephen to rescue Josie.

Chapter Twelve

✤

Desperately seeking out Stephen while trying to pretend to hang on to Porter's every word, Josie stifled the urge to tell the idiot what an insufferable ass he was. The welcoming touch of a familiar hand on her arm put her back on an even keel. Althea continued to glow while Porter held forth on the need for passing a bill to legitimize Christian prayer in public schools. Evidently Porter didn't cotton to the idea of separation of church and state.

"Darling," Stephen said in his best ever solicitous tone, "you asked me to remind you of the time. I'm sure Porter will understand, won't you, Porter?"

Porter attempted to look as if he didn't mind the interruption. Not an easy task for one so much in love with his own voice.

"My temperature, you know." Althea patted his arm to sooth his ego. "I do hope we have many more opportunities for you to share your plans with us. I'm so impressed with the scope of your interests."

Preening in his best imitation of one immune to compliments, Porter couldn't resist a parting nugget of nauseating prose. "My dearest Althea, you cannot imagine what lofty plans I have to share with you."

Oh yes she could and all of them were equally unappetizing. Turning to Stephen, she sailed out of the room on his arm, looking every inch the society icon she pretended to be.

"Jesus, Mary and Joseph." she exploded the minute they were safely in the car and out of earshot. "That man is beyond insufferable. I can't believe anyone takes him seriously. And who, pray tell, was that oily creature who sidled up to him looking like he was either going to pee his pants or bust a gut?"

"That, my sweet Althea, is no other than Elijah Flude, flunky extraordinaire, who was about to delight Porter with the splendid news that you're one step shy of being a nymphomaniac."

"Are you sure there isn't any other way, Stephen?"

"Getting cold feet, my dear?"

"Cold feet my ass." Far be it from her to admit he'd hit the nail on the head. "You try making up to that piece of slime and see how you like it."

"That's your assignment, not mine." Stephen was definitely not being supportive. "Besides, he isn't my type."

Althea punched him in the arm. "Fine support person you are. It would serve you right if I did chicken out."

"The queen of the bucket brigade?" He caught her hand in his. "Never."

What a predicament this was. Actually meeting Porter had made her face a stark reality. Scared to death didn't come close. Knock-kneed petrified was more like it.

"I need to talk to Rosemary," slipped out before she could stop herself.

"Why?" Stephen asked.

Because I need to reach out to the only anchor I've ever known. "I promised her I'd check in occasionally and it's been almost a week."

"So?"

"So, to Rosemary that's a sure sign I'm in deep doo-doo someplace and she needs to move heaven and earth to rescue me. I won't be long."

"The last time you talked to her, I swear you were on the phone for over an hour."

Josie gave Stephen her best Althea smile. "How you do go on," was followed by a limp-wristed wave as she disappeared into the front door on her way to the book-lined library.

Kicking off her shoes as she headed for one of the massive wing chairs on either side of the bay window, she took out her cell phone, punching in Rosemary's number as she sat down. The line was busy.

Drat. Now what? Confide in Stephen? No way. In spite of his unexpected confession of love, nothing had been said beyond that. She wanted to think it was because their situation controlled them. Althea and Ted must never infringe on Josie and Stephen. Okay, she was avoiding reality. She wanted a future. He lived in today. Nothing would change that. Pity. He's solid. He's caring. He's fantastic in bed. He's everything Jason wasn't. But still.

Oh, dear God, why did I have to think about Jason? It's probably because in so many ways Porter reminded me of him. An older version to be sure, and definitely no physical resemblance. Mainly it was the slick insincerity I didn't recognize in Jason until it was too late.

Tears started to form without waiting for an invitation. Not even a hint of a loss of composure was acceptable at this point. Quickly moving from the library to the foyer, Josie took the winding stairway steps two at a time. Her carefully constructed wall of composure was crumbling so fast she had all she could do to make it to the master suite. Quickly closing the door behind her, the solid wooden shield provided a welcome prop to keep her from pooling into a heap.

She punched the redial on her phone. Rosemary answered on the third ring.

"Hi," she managed, trying her best to sound composed. Not as easy feat when she was within nanoseconds of having a complete breakdown.

"What's wrong?" Rosemary demanded. "Are you sick? Are you hurt? Are you broke? Are you pregnant? No? I've got it. You're madly in love. Right?"

God bless Rosemary. The sound of her voice alone wrapped Josie in a soft blanket of comfort. Her tears forgotten for the moment, Josie laughed.

"I can't keep anything from you, can I, Rosemary? All of your worst fears are true. It's the pregnant part that's really got me. Would you believe triplets?"

"Not on your life, my precious girl. Where in the hell have you been?"

"Now, come on. I told you the training was intensive. I've been on the go like you wouldn't believe."

"And wherever that is they don't have phone reception?" Rosemary made a noise that sounded remarkably like a raspberry. "So tell me about the being madly in love part."

It was a game they played. Even through her short marriage to Jason, Rosemary asked and Josie made up the most outlandish answer she could think up on the spot.

"Let's see," she began, "he's tall, blond, sexy, gorgeous, and I'm crazy about him."

"You can do better than that," Rosemary said. "That guy who ogled you at the airport was a bloomin' stud, but definitely not your type."

Drat. How could she have forgotten Rosemary had seen Stephen?

"Oh, him," she did her best to recover. "I can see where you might have thought I was talking about him, but this guy puts him to shame. You see," she lowered her voice to a seductive whisper, "this guy's a vampire."

"Ooh. They're the rage right now I hear. You've never had one of those."

"Well," Josie went on, "you know what they say about vampires. Once bitten and all that."

Rosemary suddenly got serious. "Are you telling me you've really met someone, Josie?"

"Oh, come on, Rosemary. You know better than that. Training is way too intense to leave time for personal relationships." How was that for a bold-faced lie? "There is this one guy I'd like to get to know better, but I just don't have time for such folderol."

"You'd better make time." Happily ever after was Rosemary's favorite topic. "You're letting all of this Jason debt mess ruin your life. Speaking of Jason, his mother called for you."

Josie's heart did a one-handed back flip, landing somewhere in the vicinity of her knees. A call from Jason's mother couldn't be anything other than trouble.

"What did she want?" she asked.

"I have no idea," Rosemary said. "I didn't talk to her. It was only a message on the machine that she wanted to talk to you. She left a number. I don't suppose you want it."

About as much as she wanted a case of the mumps. "Yes and no," Josie answered honestly. Better to get it over with if possible. "What do you think I should do?"

"Considering she sounded more whiney than usual," that didn't bode well, "I'd probably vote for ignoring her. The only problem with that route is not knowing what sort of mischief she might be up to."

Precisely. "You never did trust her, did you?" Josie asked.

"Not only her," Rosemary responded. "The whole pack of 'em are a piece of work. I spent a great deal of time getting away from their ilk because I didn't want to be stuck is the same rotten pit they live in. You know how hard I wanted to believe Jason had climbed out of the world owes me mentality."

Suddenly, Althea Hartmann seemed very far away and that was unacceptable. Josie took a deep breath, willing herself to put anything personal behind her.

"Rosemary, I need a huge favor."

"You name it, sweetheart, and it's yours."

"Please call Masie Giltner for me and find out what she wants. I'm in no position right now to be dealing with anything personal. You know how to handle her much better than I. Do whatever you think is best. Tell her I've moved to Mars."

"Consider it done. The Giltner woman will be handled. As for you, young lady, when are you coming home? Don't they let you out for good behavior?"

"What makes you think I'm being good?" Josie teased.

"My God, child. You do drive me to distraction. I miss you and I worry about you traipsing about babbling Russian or Lower Slobbovian or whatever it is. You need to be here with me. Safe. Secure."

How lovely that sounded. If Rosemary only knew.

"No can do yet," she said, hanging onto the phone as if some of her godmother's strength might magically transfer into her rapidly sagging faith in herself. "As soon as there's a light at the end of the tunnel, I promise I'll let you know."

"In other words, you're saying good-bye," Rosemary sniffed,

"I'll try to call soon."

"That's what they all say. Enjoy your vampire, dear. I hope he's not too draining."

Chuckling at her own humor, Rosemary hung up. She never said good-bye, not out of rudeness, but in a fervent belief that saying it was bad luck. Cradling the now dead phone in her hand, Josie burst into hysterical tears.

She knew she was out of control. Her nerves had been wound so tightly, they had reached the breaking point. Along with her body shaking beyond any ability to stop it, each ragged sob against her lungs slowly depleted her supply of oxygen. It took several minutes before she realized Stephen was wrestling with her flailing arms in an attempt to calm her down.

"It's okay, Josie," he said over and over again. "I'm here. You're all right. Come on, now. Calm down. Tell me what's wrong."

She heard his voice as if she was on a phone with a bad connection. The only sensation that reached her was the strength of his arms holding her close to him in an effort to settle her down. Any attempt at pretense didn't have a chance. She'd broken all the rules, probably ruined the entire operation, and there wasn't a damn thing she could do about it.

"How can you have anything to do with me?" she wailed, grasping for air. "I've fallen apart exactly like you thought I would. You were right. I shouldn't have tried this. It's just that it's so much money and I've got to pay it back." Her voice had taken on a shrill quality she couldn't control. "If I had known how much Porter was like Jason, I wouldn't have even tried. I'm sorry, Stephen. I'm so sorry."

Burying her head in his chest, she tried to hide her shame. A remarkably unladylike hiccup burst from her before she could stop it. Creeping hysteria loomed like a hovering wraith waiting to pounce at the least provocation.

"Whoa, there," Stephen soothed, rocking her gently. "Back up. You've lost me. First of all, you have nothing to be sorry for. We're still on track. You'll come around. You'll see. You're going to have to explain the money part to me and how Porter and Jason got intertwined."

Josie looked up at him. She needed to see compassion rather than pity in his eyes. He was so clever at hiding his feelings, even his eyes rarely changed except in the heat of passion. Now he looked genuinely concerned. She'd settle for that.

"I'm going to guess Thaddeus gave you a capsulized version of what Jason did," she began.

"He said he was a con artist who swindled people in a phony art scheme unbeknownst to you and left you holding the bag when he killed himself."

"I'm not proud of that, Stephen. In retrospect, I see a lot of things I should have seen. He snowed me, pure and simple. I hate myself for falling for it and I hate him for what he did to all those people."

She moved out of Stephen's arms, not trusting herself to maintain her composure if she remained close to him. Hugging herself against the guilt, she paced around the bedroom while he sat down on the bed.

"What Jason did isn't your fault, Josie."

"Oh, yes it is, Stephen. Don't you see? For all intents and purposes, I might as well have been his accomplice. While he was pulling his scams, I was right there beside him helping him along. Ignorance is no excuse."

"You can't tell me anyone holds you responsible," Stephen insisted.

"I hold me responsible," she said. "And, in spite of everything, there's a segment of embassy brass that have never been convinced I wasn't somehow in on the entire scheme.

"That's preposterous."

Seeing the anger in Stephen's eyes, she faced toward him. "Not really. Look at what Porter has done. He's convinced a good number of well-meaning people to part with huge sums of money by playing on their beliefs. Jason did the same thing although he was selling an investment instead of faith. Say what you may about people who fall for a too good to be true scheme, by the very nature of my association with Jason, there was bound to be some suspicion fall on me."

Stephen stood up from the bed and walked over to her, opening his arms.

"Come here," he invited.

She walked into the welcome circle, leaning against the warm comfort he provided.

"There's no way you can ever convince me you had anything to do with what Jason did," he told her. "I admire you tremendously for wanting to pay his victims back. Now, tell me why Porter upset you so much."

"I'm not sure I can explain that very well," she said. "He and Jason really have nothing in common except an oily, slithering manner that stays somewhere under the radar where innocent people can't see it."

"You saw it in Jason, didn't you?"

"Not until after, Stephen."

"That may be your problem then." Stephen became her trainer again. "Take yourself out of the mindset. Sure, you know Porter is conning those people. That's to your advantage. Now you get to play him for the patsy. That's the beauty of it."

"It makes so much sense when you say it." she said. "Needless to say, my confidence level isn't up to par at the moment."

"That's why you have me," Stephen told her. "Now we have Porter right where we want him. You bag him. I snag him. Now, take a deep breath."

She did.

"Repeat after me." His eyes bore into hers. "I'm damn good."

In a small voice she repeated, "I'm damn good."

"Louder," he told her.

She followed his instructions just as she had back at the cabin. Slowly, she felt an inkling of confidence returning. Stephen was right. She was good. The hysteria gradually went away. The strength in his arms flowed into her.

"Promise me something, Stephen." Her voice was muffled with her mouth buried in his chest.

"You name it," he said.

"Don't ever desert me."

"You have my word, Josie. Wherever you are or whatever you're doing, I'll be right there behind you, protecting you. Nothing short of death could stop me."

Now there was an angle she hadn't considered. "Do you have a gun, Stephen?" she asked.

He looked surprised at her question.

"I have more than one at my disposal, yes."

"Do you think you may have to use one of them?" she asked.

"It's possible, Josie. That's why I had you do those exercises wearing a bullet-proof vest."

"I thought those were just to wear me down so I'd back out."

The admission made her feel like an idiot. It was obvious from the look on Stephen's face he was struggling not to come back at her with a sarcastic remark about her naiveté. Was it her fault guns scared the bejesus out of her? Never mind, recovery was essential and exactly how she was going to do that escaped her. To hide her embarrassment, she stepped away from him. A flicker of memory came back to her from her training when Stephen had explained that she was to do in the event gunplay was involved. Foolishly, she had chosen to ignore that option as a possibility.

Regrouping was in order and there was no way she could do it in the same room with Stephen. Squaring her shoulders, she met his gaze without flinching.

"I can imagine what you must be thinking." Was it possible to be smelling smoke coming out of his ears? "Please bear with me a while longer while I pick up the pieces of my shattered pride."

He made a movement toward her.

"No," she put out a hand to stop him, "please don't. I've been depending on your strength rather than my own. I'm going for a walk in the garden. Alone. When I get back, I can assure you I'll have my act together."

Mustering every ounce of courage she possessed, Josie left the room. Maybe she had mastered the finer aspects of acting after all. What she would do if she couldn't get her confidence in herself back, she had no idea.

Chapter Thirteen

❖

Watching her go, Stephen knew with complete certainty that as soon as this whole mess was over, he would resign his position and ask Josie to marry him. For the moment, he would ignore the fact that he was furious with her. She knew how dangerous the game was they were playing. How could she have forgotten? Oh, hell. He knew the answer. Unlike him, she had no prior experience to gauge what they might be up against. So she'd had a case of nerves. So be it. She'd proven herself to be one tough cookie. He had to trust she'd pull herself together.

Looking out of the window, his eyes followed her as she walked down the brick path in the garden. At the end of the path was an elaborate enclosed gazebo. There, with luck, she'd get herself back into perspective. In the meantime, he needed to listen to the cassette that had been passed to him at Porter's house.

"Moves are finally being made."

The man who had taken the name of Jonah had obviously made the recording somewhere other than at Porter's house. Stephen could hear him perfectly.

"Porter has leased two executive hangars at John Wayne Airport. They are quite sizable, providing a lot of extra room for the goodies that have been stockpiled over the years and kept in various warehouses in the LA area. The plan is to move everything to the airport hangars to be ready for transport. Until then, the warehouse addresses are as follows."

Stephen wrote down the numbers, recognizing that all of the locations surrounded the airport. When Porter was ready to move, he could easily collect his resources without drawing attention or suspicion to what was taking place.

"The operation is winding down," Jonah continued. "Apparently the bidding has narrowed down to only two players. No one except Porter knows who they are. Doesn't matter anyhow. My observations tell me this is the time he'll start to get sloppy. We have to use that to our advantage. The lovely Althea needs to work fast. He's making noises about moving the merchandise, as he calls it. I'll try to contact you with the first move date, but that may not be possible. Get the warehouses staked out pronto."

That was the end of the cassette. Stephen set fire to it, watching it burn in a large ashtray he'd gotten specifically for that purpose. As he did so, he looked toward the gazebo at the same moment Josie appeared at the door. Her posture said she was ready to kick ass.

Something told him it was just as well she hadn't heard the tape. Better she shouldn't be aware of the urgency at this point. He'd trust Porter's libido to trip him up before the weapons all made it to the hangars. Disposing of the contents of the ashtray, Stephen turned as Josie entered the bedroom. Her grin was a little lopsided, but it was firmly in place.

"Ready when you are," she said.

"Then let's get this caper wrapped up in record time," he replied, almost knocked off his feet by Josie's enthusiastic version of a bear hug.

"What's the next step, kemosabe?" she asked.

"Was the Lone Ranger good in bed?" he wondered aloud.

"Beats me," she answered, "but we sure as hell want to convince Porter that Althea will provide a sexual banquet unlike anything he's ever known in his life."

"Then let the teasing begin," Stephen announced. "By the time he has you right where he wants you, he's going to be so tired of having a permanent hard-on, he'll probably be ready to screw a light socket."

"Ouch. What do we do first?"

First were carefully arranged chance encounters designed to keep Porter dangling at the edge of thinking a tryst with Althea was almost within his grasp. While the scope of his conquests wasn't known, how he always went about snaring his next lady never varied, making him predictable. Weaving a blend of biblical references with how the woman he wanted inspired him in his work had usually gotten him what he wanted. There was more than a little suspicion he may have sometimes resorted to mood enhancements drugs of the illegal variety. With most of the women he chose, extra marital affairs were a way of life. Since no one came forward to accuse Porter of any impropriety, he had apparently been very selective. With Althea Hartmann, he had his hands full.

After the chance encounters came the let's get together just you and me game. Having firmly established that the doting Ted closely resembled a leech when it came to being with Althea, setting up a public more or less intimate occasion took some finagling. Since it was plausible that Ted would not go with Althea to have her hair done, the date was made to have lunch after her hair stylist's appointment.

Agency personnel occupied all of the tables surrounding them. The table where Porter and Althea sat was arranged in such a way he could look all he wanted, but he couldn't touch. Disguised as an elderly gentleman with a young, attractive companion, Stephen was mere feet away from Josie's chair.

"Well, isn't this just the nicest place?" Althea gushed. "Would you think badly of me if I had an itty-bitty glass of wine?"

"Not at all, my dear," Porter said, making an attempt to ooze charm. "I think I just may join you."

Stephen imagined Porter would prefer something stronger. His drink of choice was ten year old scotch.

"I can't begin to tell you how special it is to have you all to myself." Josie got right to the chase. It was a good bet her target would rise to the bait.

"My dear Althea, my admiration for you knows no bounds. You are indeed blessed among women."

Comparing her to the Virgin Mary was a stretch, but what the heck? As long as he lavished praise, he was playing into their hands.

"Why, Porter," Althea's lashes batted furiously. "That's so sweet. I swear you set my heart to racing. I'm positively vibrating with anticipation."

Offered the thread of sexual innuendo, Porter went into high gear. By the end of lunch, he had pulled out all of the stops to convince Althea how irresistible he was. Amply spurred on by what he took to be encouragement, he wasted no time plunging into the subject of where they might meet to consummate what he referred to as their heavenly union.

Now came the tricky part for Josie. Somehow she had to steer Porter toward a location conducive to assuring his arrest before he had time to lay a hand on her.

"You know," she said, smoothing out an imaginary wrinkle on the tablecloth, "ingenuity sometimes requires a large measure of originality."

"Such as?" Porter asked, practically panting with anticipation.

"We need to think outside of the box." Althea's lashes were at it again. "Or I should say go where we would not be expected to go."

"You're absolutely right, Althea." Had she suggested they tear one off right there on the table in front of everybody, he'd have agreed and hang the consequences. "I should have thought of that. Nothing ordinary will do."

"Well," she said, getting up from her chair, "you think about it and let me know. Land, air or sea." Staying where she was, she snapped her fingers as if inspiration had suddenly hit her. "Perhaps an airport. There's a thought. Now, I really must run. Oh, before I forget it, did you get my check?" Porter nodded, one step short of salivating. "I do hope it helps." Althea bestowed her tight little smile upon him. "Thank you so much for such a lovely lunch."

Carefully avoiding the hand he stretched toward her as if she didn't see it, she paused at several tables on her way out to greet acquaintances. As Althea always did, she made a spectacular exit. Stephen and his companion were directly behind. He judged Josie to be in complete control by the way she pulled out of her parking space and eased into traffic. This is not to say she didn't do one of her by now typical explosions once they were back in the safety of the master suite.

"I'm going to throw up. I swear I am. Have you any idea what it's like to sit across from that creature while he's ogling your push-up bra the whole time? Blessed among women, my ass. If he doesn't take the airport bait, I think I'll scream."

"Now, now," he soothed. "I've done some ogling myself."

"That's totally different and you know it. I must confess the only reason I got through lunch today was knowing you were right there behind me. Please give me your word that you'll always be that close."

"I can't do that, Josie. Sometimes it isn't possible. What I can do is always be sure you have the best protection possible. When you're luring Porter to his downfall, it would hardly be appropriate for me to be that close."

"Okay," she said, "I'll buy that. All I ask is that when it's all over, you'll be there."

He didn't have the heart to say it might not be possible. Their partnership had taken turns he had never expected. Instead of her pressing for permanence, it was he. He still didn't know what sort of future she wanted.

"You can bet I'll try," sounded weak, even to him. That didn't change the fact that when an assignment was over, it was over. Everyone went their separate ways. Of course, he'd be part of her backup team, but then, who knew? He was thinking way beyond what happened after Porter was put away.

How could he say that to Josie without making a commitment? If he quit his job at the agency, he'd have to find some other way of making a living. Lately, he'd been thinking a lot about the farm. Why, he wasn't sure.

He figured it was Josie's doing in an odd sort of way. Unlike him, she didn't hold grudges. Maybe it was time he let go of some of his.

"What are you thinking?" she asked.

"About home," he admitted.

"Oh? I thought we weren't supposed to do that sort of thing when we're on assignment."

"It isn't the first rule you've made me break."

"Me?" By now he was quite familiar with her wide-eyed innocent look.

"Yes, you. If we're looking for a future together, which I hope we are, I've got to be able to support you."

"Oh my," she said, truly looking surprised. "I wasn't expecting that."

"This probably isn't the best time to be talking about it," he said. "All I know is I want you in my life. Forever."

His wonderfully always composed Josie looked uncharacteristically flustered. "I don't see how that can be, Stephen. Please understand. I'm not opposed to the idea, but there's no way I can be making any commitments until I've paid off my debt."

The wrenching feeling in his gut came damn close to making him lose his temper. Her and her blasted debt. Didn't she realize he could easily pay back every penny she insisted she owed? Before he could get to that subject, he felt his cell vibrate. It was one of the agents on stakeout.

"Something's going down," the agent said. "We've got several semis lining up here and what looks like goods being transferred. Thought you'd want to know."

"Keep me informed," Stephen told him before disconnecting.

"What's up?" Josie asked.

"It looks as if Porter's starting to move stuff to the airport. Our check must have done the trick."

"Does that mean I may be off the hook for playing femme fatale?" She sounded hopeful.

"Don't count on it. He'll probably transport the stuff over a fair number of days. He won't move quickly. Knowing his modus operandi, you're filed under unfinished business and he's known for not liking loose ends."

"Then I really need a hug for luck," she said.

"I want more than a hug," he replied, wrapping his arms around her. "Damn assignments anyway."

Stephen's prediction was right on the money. A cell phone had been designated for Josie to exchange calls with Porter. To keep up the pretense Ted was with her almost constantly, she answered his increasingly frequent calls sparingly.

Evidently, he didn't cotton to the suggestion of an airport tryst. He came up with a variety of meeting places including a hot air balloon, but no airport. Meanwhile, a vast collection of weapons was moving along the interstate leading to John Wayne Airport on a daily basis. As expected, Porter never went anywhere near the hangars. It was up to Josie to lure him into meeting her at one of his rentals.

She came up with an idea that seemed their best bet for success. A recording of airport noises served as a background for her call. She told Porter that she and Ted were having their private jet redecorated to explain where she was. With Stephen right behind her, she launched into how everything from the smell of jet fuel to noisy take offs and landings were as close as she could get to an aphrodisiac. By the time she finished, she not only had Porter convinced, but Stephen as well.

Now the trick was to get Porter in a hangar loaded with his cache of weapons. Needless to say, it wasn't an easy sell. He knew being anywhere near the merchandise was a one way ticket to jail. The obvious, to him, was the hangar where the Hartmanns' plane was. Josie pointed out to him that unless he wanted a ménage a trois, that was out of the question.

Then she asked Porter if he might have someone in his wide circle of supporters that had a plane at the airport. Since that would require explanations, it was rejected. The ball was in Porter's court. If he wanted Althea, he had to risk getting caught with the goods. Any sane person would have flat out said no to such a notion. Suffused with lust, Porter's thought processes were far from objective.

"How about this?" he asked.

Stephen held his breath. He could tell Josie was doing the same.

"It just so happens I have a couple of hangars over at John Wayne Airport."

"You do?" Josie urged him on. "Whatever for?"

Had Porter possessed any sense, he would have stopped right there. He didn't.

"There's a lot you don't know about me." Porter's tone was that of a braggart. "I dabble in a number of things."

"And I'll bet you're very good at them." Josie fed his ego.

"I am indeed." Modesty wasn't one of Porter's strong suits. "If you don't mind rather Spartan surroundings, I think I have the perfect spot for us to meet."

"How intriguing." There was a definite purring sound to her voice. "Do tell me more. Are you saying it's primitive? I'm crazy about primitive."

Stephen swore he could hear Porter's voice go up in register when he answered, "Then you're going to love packing crates."

"Ooh. I've never done packing crates. How exciting. Now then," Josie added a breathless quality to her voice, "let's set a time."

Once again, leading Porter in the direction they wanted was required. He wanted cover of darkness. They wanted glaring light of day with full press coverage to chronicle the downfall of a master crook. Persuasion was Porter's stock in trade, but he was a rank amateur when it came to Josie's ability to get her own way. In a matter of minutes, he crumbled. Flushed with success, Josie turned off the phone.

"Are we good or what?" she asked.

Stephen took her in his arms, resting his head on top of hers. "I'm just along for the ride," he answered.

Chapter Fourteen

❖

Talk about jazzed. The adrenalin rush was so intense she swore she could feel it flowing through her veins. At last her confidence was restored. She could do this. No questions asked. There wasn't a doubt in her mind. Porter Holloway was dead meat.

"Things are going to get a little crazy now," Stephen told her.

"Are you trying to tell me what we've been through the past months has been normal?"

He smiled. "It may seem so when we get to the airport. Since we now know which hangar he'll be using, we can finish the subpoena process and get our people in place to be sure you have as much protection as possible."

"They'll be inside, won't they?"

"That's the plan, Josie. Keep in mind if that doesn't work out, we'll be right behind you. It probably isn't something we'll be able to communicate with you about. Your job is to get him in there with the goods. If you can get him to say something incriminating, so much the better. There will be lots of witnesses."

She couldn't help but notice the space Stephen put between them. It wasn't that he had moved away from her. He hadn't. Instead, he had assumed his professional demeanor, an aloofness she had taken for granted in the beginning. Knowing he'd be there to catch her when it was all over gave her the courage to mimic his actions. Less than twenty-four hours from now, the caper would be over.

"What happens when Porter is in custody, Stephen?"

"Generally, we all fade into the background as quickly as possible and let the agency honchos handle the limelight. There will be vans on hand to whisk us away. We'll get word on what to look for before we leave for the airport. How long the debriefing takes will be up to Thaddeus."

"Will he be there?" she asked.

"In all probability. Not in the glare of the cameras, mind you. That's for the brass. Considering it was his brainchild, I fully expect him to be in for the finish."

"I see," was about all she could manage. "I think I'll go pack my things."

Don't let your bubble burst, she cautioned herself. You knew going in this wasn't going to last. You're the one with the debt that's come between you. Hold your head up and pretend you don't care.

"Josie?"

She turned to him, hoping against hope he might relax the shield he'd put up between them."

"I'll keep you informed as best I can."

Wow. That was a real bell ringer. So much for romantic notions.

"Thanks," she said. "I'll count on it."

Deliberately walking away to her dressing room, she got out the suitcases that held her personal clothes. All she needed to add were toiletries and she'd be packed. Next came the dress she'd chosen to wear for the final meeting with Porter. Guaranteed to have him spinning out of control, its most endearing feature was an excess number of hooks and buttons to make removal as difficult as possible. The flip side of that was it took an inordinate amount of time to put on.

For what would be the last time, she turned on the vanity lights to transform herself into Althea. Her habit was to line up the large array of necessities in a very specific order so she wouldn't forget anything. Althea wore a lot more make-up than Josie did.

Once everything was arranged to her satisfaction, she left the dressing room to shower, after which she chose the proper Althea bra and skimpy panties. One of the few things she would miss about Althea was the hand stitched silk dressing gown that wrapped her body in whispering folds. She felt rather than heard Stephen enter her dressing room as she sat down to put on Althea's face.

"The vans are fire engine red with Muldoon's Maintenance signs all over them," he said, resting his hands lightly on her shoulders. "Choose any of them you can get to. The object is for us to clear the area as quickly as possible."

Their eyes met in the mirror. He was, once again, the Stephen of her dreams. Gently massaging the tight muscles in her neck, he made those darn little sexy pixies start dancing in her stomach.

Hopes are easily dashed. The faint buzz of his personal cell phone changed him back into being all business again. The impression of his hands on her shoulders lasted long after he had left the room, answering his phone as he went. She paid no attention to the murmur of voices coming from the bedroom. Her job was to finish the assignment she had agreed to do. She'd deal with the issue of Stephen later.

Ready to leave, Josie had herself psyched. There was no solicitous Ted to accompany her, but screw him. For this part of the plan, she was a solo act. Although she would pull up to the hangar in her signature silver Lexus, another agent drove her as far as the airport. Then, she was on her own. A strange calmness settled over her as she parked and got out of the car.

To the casual observer, nothing but legitimate airport business was taking place in and around the private airport hangars. Several Muldoon's Maintenance vans were parked at the hangar next to Porter's. The door of the adjacent hangar was wide open and a large number of what appeared to be mechanics were on hand. Josie supposed they were her backup team. At least she hoped they were.

Walking toward Porter's hangar, it looked quite deserted. What if he had come to his senses and realized how stupid it was to risk everything for a quickie in the hay or on packing crates to be more precise? But, oh no. As the thought occurred to her, up drove Porter in a taxi yellow Hummer. So much for being low key.

Nattily dressed for the occasion in a blue blazer and gray slacks, the abundance of aftershave lotion he had applied drifted across the space between them like a cloud of atomic dust. Not even Rosemary dared to be that generous with her overpowering scents. Josie hoped she wouldn't choke.

"Porter," she called out gaily, making every pretense of being delighted to see him.

"Althea, my pet. How charming you look."

How could he tell? His eyes were glued to her cleavage.

"Why, thank you, Porter." She considered touching his cheek or some such gesture, but couldn't make herself do it. "You're looking right sharp yourself," was the best she could do.

That appealed to his gigantic ego. His attempt at a smile came out as a leer, which she thought fit his image completely.

"Shall we?"

He indicated the direction of the hangar. Josie knew exactly how Daniel had felt going into the lion's den. Instead of using the yawning entryway door that allowed aircraft access, Porter went around to the side of the building. Fortunately for Josie's jangled nerves, it was the side closest to the companion hangar where all of the activity was.

Keying in his code to the pin pad lock, Porter finally took his eyes off of her, She almost laughed out loud when she saw he had chosen A,B,C,D as his code. All those guns and stuff being guarded by the first four letters of the alphabet. Trust him to ignore every security procedure ever printed. Evidently he'd decided he was infallible. Carefully looking around to see if they were being watched, he slowly opened the door. Then he reached inside to turn on the lights.

"After you, my dear." He made a clumsy attempt at a gallant bow.

Clenching her teeth, but giving her all in the spirit of the occasion, Josie dropped a quick curtsey before stepping over the door sill. What she saw in the glare of the vast array of overhead lights boggled her mind. The entire hangar was stacked floor to ceiling with packing crates arranged in precise rows with narrow aisles in-between.

"My goodness," she exclaimed with an appropriate hand to her mouth gesture, "you have quite a collection here. I do declare you've got enough crates here to sink a ship. Are they all yours?"

Since is wasn't likely Althea would give a rat's ass about the contents, Josie refrained from asking. Her quick perusal included a stack of crates with the notation RPG7. She was proud of herself for remembering RPG stood for rocket propelled grenade from her weapons training.

"Every one of them is mine. I own them all," Porter smugly incriminated himself. Josie figured if anyone was listening, they had what they needed for snagging him. Unfortunately, nobody popped out to snatch Porter. She was still stuck with him.

"Now you wait right here," he continued, "I have a blanket in the car. I'll go back and get it. You wait right here," he repeated as if she had a choice in the matter.

Temporarily saved by his faulty memory, Josie mimicked his smug look. "How sweet of you." She doubted sweet had anything to do with what he hoped to accomplish on that blanket.

The minute he was out of the door, she heard a "psst" from her left. "Over here, Josie," a voice whispered. Was it Stephen? "Get behind me quickly."

She followed the sound into the shadows of the aisle, unable to make out who had called to her. Immediately getting behind the shadowy figure, she knew for sure it wasn't Stephen. Swallowing her disappointment, she heard Porter returning through the door and closing it behind him.

"Freeze," a commanding voice ordered. "Porter Holloway, you're under arrest. You have the right to remain silent."

As the arresting agent continued on with the litany of his rights, Porter was screaming at the top of his voice. "I'll get you for this, you bitch. You set me up. Don't think you can hide from me, cunt. Meet me at an airport you said. I threw everything away for you. Don't think you're safe from me. I've got more fucking connections than you can count."

"That ought to play well for the press," her protector said. "Hi. I'm Jack Arden. Thaddeus asked me to be your escort out of here as soon as the scene outside settles down.

Josie shook the hand he held out to her and managed a smile. She'd no doubt meet up with Stephen later. Following Jack to the door of the hangar, a Muldoon van was parked in such a way no one could see who got into it. From what Josie could tell, the area around the hangar had turned into a three ring circus. It looked as if every major television station had a reporter and camera person on the scene. Porter's hangar was heavily guarded by no-nonsense looking guys packing big guns and an attitude that said don't mess with me.

Unaware of whom besides Jack got into the van with her, she pretended interest in the press spectacle as the driver eased through the throng. Tinted windows made it impossible for anyone to see who was in the van. She closed her eyes. Where was Stephen?

By the time the van stopped, she had a splitting headache. She was the last to get out, having no idea where they were.

"Bravo, Josie."

She would have known that voice anywhere. Looking for all the world like a disheveled gnome recovering from a three day drunk, his smile was broad and she had to admit she was glad to see him. Going into his outstretched arms, she bent down to give him a hug.

"Come with me, my dear," Thaddeus said. "We'll find a quiet place where we can talk."

They were in a large, pleasantly furnished house somewhere. By now, Josie was used to set-ups that weren't what they were supposed to be. She assumed this was another was of those.

"Where are we?" she asked.

"In Costa Mesa," he replied as if that should mean something to her. "This is as good a place as any for the debriefing."

"Debriefing?" she echoed. She had forgotten all about that.

"Depending on the scope of the operation, we sometimes schedule a debriefing afterwards. This is one of those times."

"How long will we be here?" she asked.

"Are you anxious to get home?"

Home meant no more paychecks. She had to tough it out at least through debriefing, which sounded dreary at best.

"Oh, no," she assured him. "I was just curious."

Besides, she didn't have a home. She had dreamed about having one with Stephen some day. Wherever he was. Speaking of that, "where is Stephen?" she asked, acting as nonchalant as she could.

"There was a family emergency," Thaddeus replied. "He's gone home."

"Oh?"

Without a word to her? How could he?

"His older brother passed away suddenly. Apparently the shock was too much for his father, so Stephen went home to lend a hand."

Something didn't add up here. From what Stephen had told her about his father, helping him out didn't fit. She couldn't ask. Thaddeus had no idea about her and Stephen. Or if he did, he was too cagey to mention it.

"Will he be back for the debriefing?" she asked, thinking that was a safe enough question.

"No." Thaddeus showed no reaction to her inquiry one way or the other. "He has resigned effective immediately."

He had done what? Without so much as a kiss my foot or a thank you ma'am? In the space of five seconds, her temperature went up two degrees.

"That must have come as a surprise." She tried in vain to see any emotion from Thaddeus.

"It happens." Enigmatic as ever, he reached inside his jacket and pulled an envelope out of his pocket. "He left this for you."

She took the plain white envelope from Thaddeus. Opening it was out of the question. There was no way she wanted to show her boss she cared one way or the other. Trying to concentrate on what she was being told about the debriefing process took every bit of strength she had. If Stephen Angelus thought for one minute he could get away with dumping her like yesterday's garbage, he had another think coming. From what Thaddeus was saying, her revenge would have to wait. Depending on many variables that, typical of Thaddeus, weren't explained, it might be more than a week before she could think about leaving California. So much the better. It would give her more time to formulate a plan.

When Thaddeus was finally finished with her, she was shown to a suite of rooms where she would stay to complete her assignment. She put the folder he had given to her that detailed meeting and meal times on top of her suitcase before opening the envelope from Stephen.

"I'm sorry. No time to explain. Please come to the farm. I'll be waiting for you."

A sob caught in her throat. At least he had tried. Fiddling with the hooks and buttons to get out of Althea's femme fatale outfit, Josie's brain went into overdrive. The first debriefing meeting was in an hour. It would take all of that to shed the clothes and the make-up. Then she'd figure out a way to get in touch with Stephen.

Rule number one for the debriefing duration was handed out at the first meeting. Until they were finished, no outside contact was allowed. All cell phones were collected as were laptops and all other devices. So much for reaching Stephen.

Long days and longer nights reached out in front of her. Agents, she found out, belonged to a closed society and she was not included. It was obvious to her that the others in the group thought of her much as Stephen had in the beginning. They were civil. Nothing more.

Her only amusement, besides taking long walks, was following the public details of Porter's demise on the news, both on TV and in the newspapers. It was in the later, in a small article, she read that a socialite couple, Theodore and Althea Hartmann, had been tragically killed when the pilot of their private plane inexplicably lost control over the Sierras. The story had been planted, Thaddeus told her, as an explanation for their disappearance as well as for Porter's benefit. With little else to do in his new lodgings, Porter, it seemed, read the newspaper from cover to cover. He was sure to have seen that his nemesis was dead.

She used the long walks she took to control her sanity. Railing at Stephen one minute and longing for him the next had her on an emotional merry-go-round that never stopped. The grounds of the small estate where they were staying were extensive enough to allow her about an hour in-between tedious debriefing meetings to try and collect her thoughts. Most of what went on didn't pertain to her role in the project anyway. Surely they must be almost done. In her opinion, Thaddeus had dissected the entire Althea and Ted episode to death a couple of days ago.

With an audible sigh, she started back to the main house. As she passed the fish grotto, she heard voices. Seeing who they were wasn't possible. Clearly it was a male and a female talking.

"Why do you suppose Angelus left?"

Josie came to an immediate halt. She shouldn't eavesdrop, but of course she would.

"It beats me," the male voice said. "I don't believe that crap about the brother dying."

"Why not?" the woman asked.

"I grew up not far from the Angelus spread. John Angelus might have been a lush, but he was as strong as an ox. I think Stephen couldn't take playing second fiddle to an amateur and decided to split."

Josie bristled at that remark. She'd more than proven herself, damn it.

"You could be right," the female agent said, "but what would he do? His job with the agency was like an obsession with him."

"It may have looked that way." By this time Josie thoroughly despised the guy, whoever he was. "Stephen Angelus is just like his old man. He'll find some rich broad to marry and settle down to the good life of raising thoroughbred horses."

"I heard a rumor that some people thought he had fallen for the Giltner woman."

Josie puffed right up with that bit of information until she heard his reply.

"Her?" he snorted. "She's not his type. Take my word for it. He likes them busty and petite." Instinctively Josie tried to make herself shorter as she looked down at her less than well-endowed chest. "The racing folks don't mingle outside of their set. Oh, he may have led her on to get a free piece of ass. That wouldn't surprise me. They were, after all, playing house. No, you can take my word for it. He couldn't wait to get out of here. He didn't even wait until Porter was bagged. No sir. He left that woman high and dry and caught a morning flight is what I heard."

Josie started walking quickly to put as much distance as possible between herself and the pair at the grotto. Not his type, huh? What did that guy know? He was just mouthing off. Then again, on the other hand, what if he was right? No. She wouldn't believe it. Correction. She couldn't believe it. She'd go to the farm all right and see for herself. Bristling with righteous indignation, she headed toward the house for what turned out to be the final session at last.

Packing her bags was a piece of cake. She had never unpacked. Checking the room to be sure she hadn't left anything personal, she heard a knock at the door. Thinking it was someone to get her bags, she called out, "come in."

"May I have a minute?" Thaddeus asked, appearing around the door.

Looking as rumpled as ever in his ill-fitting suit, Josie wondered if she'd ever see him again after today. "Please," she said, "come in."

"I won't take long," he assured her. "Charles Montague wanted me to give you this."

Good old Charles who had told her not to take being put out of a job personally. The very one Rosemary wanted to string up by his balls. She took the paper Thaddeus handed to her. It was the promissory note she had signed to pay off Jason's debt. Surely there must be some mistake. Someone had stamped paid in full on it.

"Who?" she started.

"We don't know, Josie. Someone sent a draft to Charles with instructions to pay the remainder of your note. Whoever it was wished to remain anonymous."

And she had a damn good idea who that was. How dare he? Was that his clumsy way of kissing her off? Fat chance.

Drawing on strength she didn't know she had left in her, Josie gave Thaddeus her best Althea smile. "Thank you," seemed to be all that was required.

"I suppose this is good-bye then," he said.

"Yes," she answered. "I think I'll look for a line of work that's a little easier on my nerves."

He handed her an airplane ticket and her cell phone. "If you ever change your mind, let me know. It's been a pleasure having you on board. Jack will be along shortly to get your bags."

"That's okay," she replied. "I can handle them. Just steer me in the right direction."

"The vans are parked out at the front curb," he said. "The one at the front of the line is going to LAX. I booked you for Dulles. Have a safe trip and once again, thank you for your hard work."

With a small salute, he was gone. Collecting her bags, Josie said good-bye to her career as a spy.

She could call Rosemary from the airport. Then, as soon as possible, she'd get to what Stephen called the farm. After all, he had asked her to come hadn't he? Quickly checking her ticket to see what airline she was booked on, she saw a post-it note attached to a first class ticket.

Thaddeus had written, "this one's on me."

Chapter Fifteen

As soon as she got Josie's call, Rosemary immediately went into overdrive with a long list of plans she'd concocted for Josie's return.

"Don't get too carried away," Josie cautioned her. "I'm only going to be at your house overnight."

"Don't be silly," Rosemary scolded. "You've got to stay at least a week. Has that damn Muldoon creature scheduled you for another one of his droll wild goose chases?"

"No, we've actually parted company," Josie said. "I have something very important I have to do tomorrow. May I borrow your car?"

"Maxwell will take you anywhere you want to go, child."

"This is something I have to do alone, Rosemary."

"Well, that sounds mysterious. What are you up to?" Rosemary's curiosity was completely unabashed.

"I have a score to settle with someone. It's a long story," Josie told her.

"How exciting. Does it have anything to do with you dumping Muldoon? Tell me all."

"I didn't dump Muldoon, Rosemary, and I can't talk right now." Josie knew she was avoiding the inevitable. "My flight number is being called. We'll talk when I get there and remember, no plans. Okay?"

That had about as much chance as a baby coming out of the womb potty trained. By tomorrow morning, Rosemary would have guest lists galore, menus, and party themes all made up. It was her nature. Some things never changed. Of course, Josie reflected, by tomorrow night, she might be glad for the diversion. Especially if that sanctimonious bore in the grotto had been right about Stephen.

What a mess she had gotten herself into. On the one hand, her heart said Stephen loved her and had only broken his promise because he had no choice. On the other hand, there was that pesky nagging doubt that everything had been an act with him from the start to no good-bye finish. He had asked her to come to the farm, which was exactly what she planned to do. And when she was done with him, he'd rue the day he'd decided to play her for a sucker.

She was so busy plotting her revenge, not even some rather severe turbulence fazed her. Whatever the outcome was, she had to admit she was a much stronger woman than she had been on the return trip from Paris. Even flying wasn't as bad as it had been.

In flowing shocking pink with a matching turban from which diamonds dripped in wild profusion, Rosemary had already made her presence known by the time Josie got to the luggage area. Having checked her cell phone for messages on the way from the plane, the fact that Stephen hadn't even tried to reach her increased her blood pressure to new highs. Had he magically appeared at that moment, she would have cheerfully sucker punched him in the stomach and thoroughly enjoyed it. Instead of Stephen, with a long suffering Maxwell in tow, Rosemary engulfed Josie is voluminous yards of chiffon.

"My baby's home at last."

Maxwell and Josie exchanged a wink.

"You're looking well," he said, making no attempt to hide his frank appraisal of his employer's godchild. "Whatever it was you were doing, it appears to have agreed with you."

If he only knew. "Thanks, Maxwell. I see the dragon lady still has you in her clutches."

That remark produced one of his rare smiles. "I'm seriously considering retirement."

"Oh, pooh," Rosemary chimed in. "You're hardly broken in yet. Let's get Josie home."

Because she knew Maxwell would listen in on their entire conversation, Rosemary refrained from asking Josie any questions. Evidently, she decided it was all right if Maxwell heard about personal business involving the call she had returned to Josie's erstwhile mother-in-law.

"Before I forget, I want you to know I called that Giltner woman for you."

"I'm sure she was thrilled to hear from you," Josie said.

"By the time I finished with her, she was thoroughly trashed," Rosemary answered, looking extremely pleased with herself. "You'll never believe what she wanted."

"Never in a million years," Josie admitted, waiting with baited breath for what Rosemary would say.

"Well," Rosemary drew the word out for dramatic effect, "hold onto your hat. That brazen hussy had the nerve to solicit any and all offers anyone might want to make for a marble headstone to put on Jason's grave."

"He doesn't have a grave," Josie reminded her. "His mother insisted his ashes be scattered as I recall."

"You and I both know the whole headstone thing is nothing more than a ploy for money. Never you mind," Rosemary patted Josie's hand. "I set her straight in record time. Especially when she flat out said she was sure you would want to contribute."

Josie almost choked, she was laughing so hard. "Me?" she finally managed to say.

"Can you believe it? I put the brakes on that, let me tell you, in no uncertain terms. I asked her how she could feel that way when you were off on a life threatening mission to try and pay back the money her son stole. Actually, I think I said you had joined the foreign legion because it paid so well."

"My, my. You did lay it on."

"I figured she's so damn dumb she wouldn't know the difference. She didn't. All she said was she thought I would have taken care of that. It went right over her head when I said you had refused my offer of help."

Josie decided not to tell Rosemary about the debt being paid. Instead she turned her fury on Stephen for being such a jerk about not considering her feelings. Rosemary probably wouldn't have heard her anyway. She was on a roll.

"Having set her straight on that, I launched into what would happen to her if she ever tried to bother you again."

"Did it involve tar and feathers or did you just guillotine her and have it over with quickly?"

Maxwell's dry chuckle from the front seat was positive proof he'd heard every word of the conversation. Rosemary ignored him.

"Nah," Rosemary scoffed, "I hit her where I knew she'd get the message, beginning with welfare fraud and ending with exposing her husband's illegal moonshine operation to the folks at Alcohol, Tobacco and Firearms. Believe it or not, she hung up on me. Kind of pissed me off. I wanted to hang up on her. At least you're rid of that piece of white trash."

Then, as only she could when she felt a subject was closed, Rosemary spent the rest of the ride discussing many subjects, all of which revolved around her. Josie wasn't required to participate, so she didn't. Instead, she continued her scheming of how her visit with Stephen would go. Wouldn't Rosemary just die if she knew the truth?

Fortunately, even Rosemary hadn't been able to throw together her usual casual gathering including umpteen of her closest friends for dinner on such short notice. They went to the country club instead. As only he could, Wendall controlled the conversation, depriving his wife from grilling Josie. How much he knew about her recent caper was anyone's guess. Suffice it to say he was sympathetic to his godchild's need for privacy.

Watching Rosemary contain herself was a sight in itself. Evidently, Wendall had laid the groundwork with infinite care. As delighted as she was to be spared, Josie couldn't help but feel sorry for her godmother.

When it was obvious Wendall had more or less run out of things to keep the conversation flowing, Josie decided to take pity on Rosemary.

"Tell me," she said, "do either of you know anything about the Angelus race horse operations?"

"Now," Rosemary pounced, "where in the world did that come from? I knew Marie Angelus quite well. She was a saint. As for Andrew, well, we lost touch after she died. I should feel sorry for him now, I suppose, losing his older boy so suddenly. Why do you ask?"

At least Stephen's brother's death was confirmed. "I've become acquainted with the other son," she said with understated precision.

"I really never knew the boys," Rosemary admitted. "What do you mean by acquainted?"

"Just that," Josie answered evasively, thinking Rosemary was better off not knowing all of the details. "He invited me to visit the farm. That's why I want to borrow your car."

"There's something you're not telling me," Rosemary figured out in record time.

In a surprise move. Wendall laid a restraining hand on his wife's arm. "I'm sure Josie will fill us in when the time is right, my dear." Then he turned to Josie. "To answer your question, the Angelus family has the finest stable of horses there is to be had. Countless champions. Several Derby winners. The death of John Angelus was a heavy blow to the family business. As I understand it, Andrew had a major stroke when he was told John had died. I believe the younger boy, a man by now, I know, immediately came to the rescue. He and his father have been estranged for years."

Well, that filled in some gaps. So far, the jerk in the grotto was losing and Stephen was winning. "How large an operation are we talking about here, Wendall?"

"Huge, If memory serves me. It's been years since I was there, you understand. Would have gone to John's funeral, of course, had there been one."

"How huge is huge?" Josie asked.

"Oh, hundreds of acres, more or less, would be my guess. Large hilltop house with spectacular views. There's a gatekeeper's cottage, if I remember correctly and an expansive barn, of course. I think there's an apartment attached to it. Then, there are riding trails, a cross country course, and an area for jumping and dressage."

Josie slowly let all that Wendall had told her sink in. Okay, so Stephen was filthy rich. She already knew that. For the moment she would ignore the fact that she didn't know diddly about horses, racing or what in the heck dressage was. Also, what he called the farm was more precisely a vast estate. Ignoring her shallow breathing that was progressing rapidly with each passing minute, she looked first at Wendall and then at Rosemary.

"To give you a brief overview as to why I asked about the Angelus family, I recently have become intimately involved with Stephen, the younger son."

Wendall, as always, was impassive. At the mention of the word intimate, Rosemary's eyebrows shot up close to her hairline. She did not, however, say anything. Josie figured she was in a state of shock.

"By tomorrow night, I'll be able to tell you precisely what, if any, future I have with him. If you don't mind," she pushed back her chair, "I'd really like to get a good night's sleep. I'm exhausted."

In total silence, the three of them exited the dining room. Their ride to the house was also devoid of conversation. Other than a "good night and sleep well," from Rosemary, nothing more was said. It was a given poor Wendall would be the target of all her frustrations well into the wee hours. Josie expected to toss and turn all night. Instead, she slept like the proverbial rock.

The morning was clear with plenty of sunshine to bolster Josie's sagging spirits. Wendall, of course, had gone to his office while it was still dark. Nothing could coax Rosemary out of bed before ten unless it involved being required to do so in order to make an early flight for a fabulously expensive vacation. Her black Mercedes was parked in front of the house. The keys were in the ignition. Attached to the steering wheel were directions to Stephen's home.

By the time she arrived at the stately mansion that looked like a prop for Gone with the Wind, she had revved her dander up to top speed. There was no one at the gate house. Parking in the middle of the circular drive, she marched up to the front door with single minded purpose and rang the bell.

As if she was expected, the door was immediately opened by an elderly man who had faithful retainer written all over him.

"May I help you?"

The treble of his soft voice would have betrayed his age if his looks had not. Josie guessed he was close to ninety.

"I'm here to see Mr. Angelus," she stated firmly, sweeping passed him with typical Althea aplomb. "You don't need to announce me."

It occurred to her as she left the butler standing in the doorway that she didn't have the vaguest idea where she was going. The appearance of yet another elderly gentleman, this one supported by a walker, saved her from wondering where to go. The resemblance was astonishing. Stephen and his father looked exactly the same.

"Hello," she said. "I'm Josie Giltner. Could you be so kind as to tell me where I might find Stephen?" She didn't add, the bastard, in deference to the fact she was talking with his father.

A pair of piercing brown eyes topped by bushy white hair examined her thoroughly before he spoke. "He's expecting you," he said, carefully pronouncing each word. A result of his stroke perhaps. "He's out in the barn."

"Thank you," she replied, not quite sure how to react to the fact she was expected.

"Rupert can show you the way," he said, indicating the butler still standing by the door. Rupert looked appalled by the idea.

"That won't be necessary," she told him. "I'll find my own way."

Once again, she had blundered into not knowing what the way might be, but when she entered the estate, she had seen what appeared to be a barn set back from the house at a discreet distance. Choosing a path she hoped would get her to where she wanted to be, Josie quickly left Rupert and Mr. Angelus behind.

"She's going to give me some fine grandsons," Andrew said to Rupert.

"Yes suh," Rupert answered, with a look that clearly showed he had no idea what his employer was talking about.

※ ※ ※

Feeling satisfied with himself, Stephen gave one last glance at the chestnut colt that was still working on the business of keeping its feet. It had been many a year since he had assisted at a birth. If anything, the thrill had been sweeter this time. Why, he wasn't sure unless it was something else he could share with Josie. Speaking of which, where was she? Had he screwed up by leaving the way he did? The choice had to be hers. Either she loved him or she didn't. It was as simple as that.

As he reached for his shirt, he glanced toward the house. Finally. There she was, striding across the lawn with her hair flying in all directions. He stepped through the door so she could see him, waving as she approached. His own special Josie, as anxious to see him as he was to see her.

"You son of a bitch."

Yep, she was glad to see him all right. Well, maybe a little reluctant.

"Hi, you," he said. "I thought you'd never get here."

"Never get here?" she repeated. "After you left me to go through all that debriefing crap alone? How could you?"

Okay, she had some issues. A lot of tenderness was in order and if necessary, ingratiating himself.

"Come here," he said, needing to hold her reluctant body next to his. Knowing better than to try and kiss her, he temporarily satisfied himself by burying his nose in the softness of her hair, breathing in her special scent.

"Because I love you," he answered.

She pulled back a little to look at him, but stayed in his arms. "You have a very strange way of proving that."

He brought her back to him. "The ball is in your court, Josie. I've never made a secret of my feelings, but I've never been totally sure about yours. I mean, you've never told me that you love me."

That got her attention. She squirmed for him to release her, but he refused to let her go.

"How can you say such a thing, Stephen? Did you think I made love to you because I was just had the hots for you?"

A smart aleck remark back to her died in his throat. Now was not the time.

"Say it, Josie. I want to hear the words."

He felt the fight in her start to waver. Gently pressing his lips to her forehead, he repeated. "Say it, Josie."

"Even when I hated you, I think I loved you," she admitted. "The problem wasn't that and you know it. All I want to know is why you had to pay back the rest of what I owed. You know how I felt about that."

Clearly something had happened about the money for which she felt responsible. What that was, he had no idea.

"I swear I didn't do anything, Josie."

"I got a paid note from Thaddeus as I was leaving LA."

"That well may be, Josie, but I didn't have anything to do with it."

"Then who did?" she asked.

"I did."

Neither of them had heard Andrew as he entered the barn in his battery operated wheelchair.

"As I saw it that was the only obstacle between the two of you that needed to be overcome." Although his speech was slightly slurred, he managed to get the words out. "Before I die, I want a grandson, damn it."

"You might have said something to me, Dad."

"What good would that have done? You told me Josie didn't want your help. You didn't say anything about mine."

Josie relaxed then. "It's done now, Stephen." She turned to Andrew. "Thank you."

"Consider it a wedding present from a grateful old man."

"You're as full of it as he is," she told him, "and I don't want either of you to think you can get away with anymore of your shenanigans."

Stephen checked out the not so innocent look on his father's face, "I told you she would be a handful," he said, pulling Josie more securely against him.

Andrew smiled broadly until a sharp voice behind him invaded the happy scene.

"Mister Angelus. What in the name of all that's holy do you think you're doing?"

An agitated woman in a white uniform appeared in the doorway. Slightly out of breath, she glared at Andrew.

"Let me introduce you to my own personal harpy, Josie," he said. "She is supposed to be an angel of mercy. Her name is Adelaide and she is singlehandedly trying to push me into an early grave."

With a cursory nod in Josie's direction, Adelaide firmly turned Andrew's wheelchair around. "I'm doing no such thing and you know it. Just what do you think you're doing coming out here without any regard to getting a chill?"

"Quit talking to me like a baby, woman. I'm talking to the bride and groom.

"I don't care if you're talking to the president of the United States." Clearly Adelaide was not a romantic. "We're taking you back to the house. Now."

"She always seems to think there's more than one of her," Andrew explained. "I could understand if she had a robust figure, but as you can see, she's sort of a dried up prune."

Ignoring his description, Adelaide started pushing Andrew toward the house.

"See you later," he called back to them.

Josie settled her arms around Stephen's neck and said, "so that's the crabby old fart you couldn't stand?"

"There's a story there to be sure," Stephen admitted. "I would never have left you behind if I hadn't known you would be safe and if the situation hadn't been so serious. John was dead and my dad was unconscious. There wasn't anyone available to take charge except me. I knew getting to you was out, so sitting beside my father in the hospital, I told him all about you. I had no idea he could hear me. When he regained consciousness, he did his best to ream me out. Luckily for me, he couldn't talk very well at that point. The strange thing was, what he was trying to tell me was not to make the same mistakes he did."

"I don't think you ever could," Josie said. "I'm sorry about your brother."

"He was a walking time bomb, but my father didn't know it. Oh, he knew about John's drinking. What he didn't know was about the cancer John was diagnosed with a year ago. I was sworn to secrecy and honored my brother's request. Right before you and I met, he told me he was considering an aggressive chemo program that would either kill him or cure him. Unfortunately, the odds weren't in his favor."

Josie's eyes that so often mirrored her thoughts reflected her reaction to his words. She didn't speak, but held him more closely.

"I'm not saying the old man you just met has turned into a saint," he continued. "What he has done is taken a hard look at his mortality. To be honest, I shudder to think what he might be like fawning over grandchildren."

"Now there," Josie said, running her finger down his exposed chest to the only button he had managed to get fastened, "is a subject we need to discuss further. However," she cut him off before he could interrupt, "there's something else we need to talk about first."

"Do you want me on top or you?" he asked.

"Stop that," she said swatting at him. "First comes the wedding. Next comes where are we going to live. Then we get to the kids."

"Okay, I'll be serious," he promised. "You decide on the wedding, I'll make arrangements to have a house built for us, and we'll work on the kid angle together."

"Fair enough." She purposefully started slowly moving against him, easily getting him aroused. "Between Rosemary and your father, a small wedding is probably doubtful. We'll survive. My only request for the house is a winding staircase. I've always wanted one of those. As for the kids, you know what they say."

"What?"

"Practice. Practice. Practice."

"I have just the place in mind to work on that," he said, hoping to God he didn't make a fool of himself by coming before they got their clothes off.

"It isn't very far away, is it?"

He took that to mean she was as anxious as he. Looking toward the hay loft, he kissed her lightly on the lips and took her hand.

"Follow me up the ladder," he said.

"Is that what I think it is?" she asked, following along right behind him.

"Think of it as a hayride without the wagon."

"Stephen?"

"Yes?"

"I love you."

He reached the loft and pulled her up beside him. "Ah, Josie," he said, looking down at her, "I am a lucky man."

Epilogue

Twelve Years Later

Josie sat back on her heels, smoothing out a final panel in the quilted skirt encircling the bottom of the Christmas tree. The quilted skirt, along with many of the ornaments on the tree, had been carefully packed away by Marie Angelus, the mother-in-law Josie never knew. All of the holiday decorations had been stored in the treasure trove attic carefully catalogued by the woman Andrew talked about as if she was still alive. In fact, Josie sometimes thought she was, he described her so well. Of course, all she had to do was look at her oldest child, named for his grandfather, who looked remarkably like the slender, elegant woman frozen in time by so many of her portraits on the walls of the big house.

The big house, as they called it, according to Stephen, was Andrew's living mausoleum. Still going strong at ninety-two, the elder statesman insisted on rattling around in the place, amply supported by a caring staff who catered to his every whim. He would often visit the house Stephen had built for Josie, but he rarely stayed for meals and never overnight. All of his visits were designed as doting sessions for the three grandchildren he showered with affection and special attention he had sorely neglected providing for his own sons.

Andy had arrived first, almost exactly nine months to the day after the wedding of the century, accompanied by fanfare usually associated with royalty. Whatever excess Rosemary couldn't come up with, Andrew did. Josie's favorite memory of the event was in a carefully preserved picture of the long-suffering Maxwell holding her first born with the assurance of a pro.

What the picture didn't show was Rosemary screaming in the background, "if you dare drop that child, I'll have your hide."

Wendy arrived three years later, named for Josie's beloved godfather, Wendall, who had bowed out of this world without any warning a month before her birth. Needless to say, Rosemary, who planned her entire life down to the last detail, had taken great exception to his unexpected departure. In a twist of fate no one could have predicted, her many visits to see her grandchildren resulted in a quiet family wedding completely unlike the lavish affair she had planned for her godchild. As only he could, Andrew had courted Rosemary with such determination she couldn't say no. Selling her home, she dragged Maxwell and his wife along to supplement the big house staff. She would heartily have approved that Maxwell insisted he would drive the hearse when she succumbed to a heart attack after five years as Andrew's wife.

The third of Josie's and Stephen's children, who had just turned four, was named Rosemary Marie, but since birth she had been called Rosie. Although he would have vehemently denied it, she was Andrew's favorite, mainly because she had appointed herself to be his eyes, having heard his vision was failing. In truth, glasses corrected the situation for the most part, a fact not communicated to Rosie. Turning around, Josie saw the two of them standing hand in hand in the doorway looking at the tree.

"Well," she said, "what do you think?"

"It's just so prettyful," Rosie declared, being prone to invent her own vocabulary. "Where's my ormenant?"

"That's ornament," her grandfather whispered to her as she led him closer to the tree.

"Here it is," Josie said, pointing to a purple angel with a chartreuse halo Rosie had produced at pre-school in time for Christmas. Like the woman for whom she was named, Rosie had a very diverse sense of color.

"Where's Andy's?" the child asked.

Josie pointed out a lopsided camel with a green nose carefully hung between Wendy's offering that was supposed to be matching aluminum foil icicles, although one was much larger than the other. Above them was a silver bell with a diamond teardrop clapper that was engraved, Steven's and Josie's First Christmas. It had been a gift Rosemary swore was Wendall's idea. Josie knew better.

"So, I guess that's it," Josie said, standing up. "We're as decorated as we're going to be."

"Every year is always better than the last," Andrew told her.

"You," she replied, poking him gently in the chest, "are full of it."

"Full of what, Mommy?" Rosie asked.

"Full of charm and a master of all things grand and glorious," Stephen said, striding into the room and scooping Rosie up in his arms, "just like me."

"I don't know about that," Rosie said somberly, still not totally grasping family relationships such as the fact Andrew was Stephen's father. "Pop Pop is one of a kind. He told me so."

"That he is," Stephen agreed, putting his daughter down to take his wife in his arms. "And you," he said to Josie, wiggling his eyebrows so only she could see, "are prettier today than you were the day I met you."

Andrew didn't miss the eye roll. "Rosie, my girl," he said, taking his granddaughter's hand, "I think it's time you took me back home."

Watch for WHEN DREAMS ENDURE, the sequel to DARE TO DREAM
COMING SOON

Chapter One

Callie Sullivan had never felt as badly as she did today. Whoever the idiot was who wrote that stupid book, "The Joys of Pregnancy," either had a screw loose or was a man disguised as a woman. Trying to find a comfortable position was impossible. Her ankles were swollen, her belly was humongous, and her temper was at the boiling point. Struggling to get out of her chair (another problem best not discussed), she waddled toward the kitchen in search of something blessedly decadent to improve her mood. Ah, there was a silver lining. Austin was making a double fudge chocolate cake.

Austin. How could she describe him? Officially, he was an employee who tended to every need her husband, Ryan, ever imagined he might have. In actuality, he was Callie's best friend. She had, of course, never told him that. Girls born in the backwoods of West Virginia, who aren't socially conscious, rarely marry wealthy men regardless of the circumstances.

Meeting Ryan Sullivan had been pure chance. Now, she admitted, a very lucky meeting. At the time, she had been so frightened he'd unmask her ignorance, she did her best to avoid him. Now, she couldn't live without him. And wasn't it just too convenient that Austin was part of the package?

"That looks yummy," she said, preparing to dip her finger into the gooey frosting.

"Don't even think of it," Austin said sternly, softly swatting her finger away. "You can't afford to put on one more ounce if you're going to stay on the weight plan the doctor has asked you to maintain."

"The man's a sadist," Callie pouted, making another attempt to steal some icing.

"Not too long ago, you thought he was brilliant," Austin observed, staying her finger from its course. "What happened?"

"Seven more months of pregnancy and fifteen pounds reduced his status considerably. Now, I simply tolerate him. I'm making the supposition that he's best taken at face value. It's probably too late to change now."

"You'll do just fine," Austin assured her. "You have a husband who adores you and thinks you're beautiful no matter what, and even the royal bitch has softened just a tad."

The royal bitch was Ryan's mother, Leticia. Callie had to admit her mother-in-law was best taken in small doses.

"How do you think I should handle the dreaded naming of the baby?" she asked.

"Just as you have been," he replied. "Don't let her wear you down. She'll wheedle and deedle forever. You know that. In her mind, not wanting to know the sex of the baby ahead of time is unheard of and topping that off with no chosen names really burns her hide." Austin rubbed his hands together. "I love it."

"Well," she said, eyeing the frosting with longing, "we have discussed names."

"I wouldn't tell Leticia that," Austin advised.

"Oh, don't worry, but it might be nice to talk to someone about it."

"How about me?" Austin asked.

"Do you truly have an interest, Austin? I thought you might be dreading the baby. You've never said."

Callie knew Austin well enough to realize she had tapped into a part of him he hid behind the bland façade that almost never showed any emotion. It was his "servant's" face she had rarely reached beyond. Nothing ventured, she thought, waiting to see if he would say something without being prodded.

"It's probably not my place," he said predictably.

"Oh, Austin," she said. "This is us talking. You know all about me. I'm just a hick Ryan bought to be his wife."

"That may be true," Austin replied. "What you aren't mentioning is how quickly he fell in love with you and corrected his mistake with a church ceremony while you were in Ireland."

"You came all the way there to see it, Austin. I haven't forgotten. You were even kind enough to endure Leticia. Heaven knows she was a package to handle."

"Some things are best not mentioned," he cautioned her. "Leticia was out of her element in Ireland. She didn't have anyone to boss around."

Callie smiled, reaching out to touch Austin's arm. "You saw to that. Is it so hard for you to say how much you care for Ryan?"

Now Austin really looked pained, or perhaps flustered was more like it. "It's not my place," he repeated.

"You've been with Ryan ever since he came to this country from Ireland, Austin. He was twelve years old and scared to death. You can't be with someone that long and not have some kind of feeling."

"There's so much you don't understand," he said, looking off to some distant spot she couldn't see. "It wasn't I who saved Ryan. It was the other way around."

Totally intrigued, Callie hoped no one else would come into the kitchen. She had never been as close to Austin as she was at that moment.

"Is that why you're willing to have me talk about the baby?" she asked. "I mean, do you have any thoughts as to what it will be like when there's a little one around?"

Austin carefully placed the iced cake on its stand and put the covering lid over it. Then he sat down at the table across from Callie.

"Since I knew there would be a baby in the house, I've thought of little else," he said. "You see, many years ago, my wife and I had a baby. Her name was Fiona."

"Your wife?" Callie asked. Somehow she had never envisioned Austin having a wife.

"Yes," he said, his rigid facial features transforming into a softness Callie had never seen. "Her name was Sara. She, too, was Irish."

"Then, how......" she started without knowing where to finish.

"I didn't begin life as a man's servant," Austin told her. "I was a teacher at a high school right here in New York City. Sara was a fellow teacher. We fell in love, got married, and in due course, had Fiona. Ours was a simple, happy life with few luxuries, but many blessings."

Without hearing the next part of Austin's story, Callie knew there was no happy ending. Rather than speak, she let him continue.

"I had no way of knowing Sara had an abusive relationship before we met. She never spoke of it. On what would have been Fiona's first birthday, I arrived home from work to find the apartment crawling with police. My Sara was dead and so was my child. They had been murdered by the man she spurned. He had also killed himself."

Tears ran down Callie's face as she reached across the table to cover Austin's folded hands with hers. She looked into the face of a man who had always been so formal with her and was now unashamedly letting her see his grief.

"Does Ryan know?" she asked.

"No, you're the only one in the family I've told. I was hoping to convince you I could be of some help with your baby."

Somehow, the picture of Austin cradling a baby in his arms or changing a diaper wouldn't come into focus. She was still adjusting to his story.

"You've touched on a subject I'm still wrestling with," she told him. "Obviously, Leticia wants me to have a nanny for the baby, but I'm against it. Ryan worries I won't be able to juggle working along with being a mother and a wife."

"And can you?" Austin asked.

"I truly don't know," she admitted. "It's one of those we'll have to see things. Tell me, Austin. What was Ryan like as a boy? How ever did you end up working for the Sullivan's?"

"That," he said, "is a long story."

"You won't let me eat your cake," she told him. "The very least you can do is amuse me."

"Okay, Callie, I will."

Austin never called her Callie except when they were alone. She understood why.

"As you can well imagine, I was too much in shock at first to function. Then, I went into a depression so deep my doctor doubted I would ever recover. My doctor, by the way, was Sean Sullivan, the brother of Seamus, Ryan's father."

"I didn't know Ryan's father had a brother."

"He died years ago, but it was he who suggested I could best handle my grief by adopting a new identity where I kept the same name, but totally changed everything else. Don't ask me why, but somehow it appealed to me to take on the job of molding a young man into a gentleman. I was, remember, a teacher by profession. Becoming a servant didn't bother me. From a financial standpoint, I'm in much better shape than I would have been otherwise. Regretfully, I have no one to share it with."

"But surely, Austin, you have a life outside of being here with us. Don't you?"

"I do," he admitted, "but to be truthful, I don't crave companionship. I am fulfilled with what I have here. When I was raising Ryan, I didn't have time for much else. He was, as you know, the object of his father's cruelty along with coming from dire poverty. The adjustment he had to make when the Sullivan's adopted him was huge."

"Ryan rarely mentions his days before we met," Callie said. "He does, however, credit his mother with always being his champion."

"Lord knows Leticia has more than her share of bad habits. Ryan is right, though, that she's always been there for him. Make no mistake, mind you. She's no mother of the year. Motherhood is something she's always done on her own terms. My job, if you will, was to fill in the gaps, and trust me, there were a lot of gaps."

"Such as?" Callie asked.

"Consider a boy plucked from severe poverty suddenly being thrust into extreme wealth. Where once there had been nothing, all of a sudden anything he wanted was spread out in front of him. The chances of him becoming insufferable were high. Instead, the exact opposite happened. I'd like to take credit for that, but I can't."

"I'll bet I know," Callie said.

"Do you now?" Austin asked.

"You have to remember, Austin, I'm a child of poverty too. There's one influence in our lives that usually shapes us if we're lucky."

"And that is?"

"Our mothers. Their love is so fierce, no matter where we are, it guides us. I know how much Ryan loved his mother. He brought her with him in his heart when he came here from Ireland, of that, I'm sure."

"You're right, of course," Austin agreed. "My job was to mold him in other ways. His brogue was so thick, it was difficult at times to understand him and his manners beyond please and thank you were non-existent, to say nothing of his schooling."

"Gosh," Callie burst out, "it must have been like Pygmalion all over again."

"Good analogy," Austin replied, "with a lot of differences. Leticia expected miracles, you see, and I only had six years to accomplish what normally takes twelve. When one adds in I had to correct all of the snob drivel Leticia tried to drum into Ryan, it was touch and go at times."

"And so it could be said you created Ryan," Callie observed.

"No," Austin disagreed, "he learned how to create himself. That's what makes him unique."

Callie looked up at the kitchen clock, realizing it was about time for Ryan to come home. Regardless of how frumpy she felt, arranging herself into some semblance of the woman he expected her to be was in order.

"I'm going to change my clothes," she told Austin, casting one last hungry look at the chocolate cake. "Ryan should be home soon."

"You look especially nice in that green frock," Austin observed.

"That's only because Armand designed it," she reminded him.

Austin made no attempt to hide his contempt for the man who had given an untrained designer a place in the renowned House of Zolander. "Your employer," he sniffed, "gets every decent idea he has from you."

"Somehow," she reminded him as she struggled to her feet, "he managed to create the most prestigious fashion house in New York long before I got there."

"It's beyond me how he manages to have the good sense to get up in the morning," Austin quipped. "Speaking of getting up, do you need any help?"

Finally gaining her feet, Callie shook her head. "I think I'm good," she said. "If you hear a crash, you'll know I've gotten myself into trouble."

"Shall I call for Emma?" he asked, once again in his role as manager of the household.

"Yes, thank you," she told him, knowing full well without the help of her trusted maid, she'd never manage to get herself together properly.

As she reached the bedroom, a stab of pain went through her. For a moment, she couldn't move. Clutching the frame of the door, Callie waited for the moment to pass. As soon as it had, another spasm went through her, more intense than the first. Gasping for breath, she was vaguely aware of Emma hurrying down the hall toward her.

"Get Austin," she managed to say. "I think the baby is coming."

ABOUT THE AUTHOR

Ginny was born and raised in Wilmington, Delaware. A graduate of Wilson College in Chambersburg, PA, she moved to California and pursued a career in banking. She lives in Discovery Bay with her husband, Doug, and their extremely spoiled cats, Amos and Andy.

She loves to hear from her readers. Visit her at www.ginnyvermillion.net

Other Books By Ginny

Dare To Dream

Made in the USA
Lexington, KY
15 July 2013